The Reinvention *of* Ivy Brown

Also by Roberta Taylor:

Too Many Mothers

Roberta
TAYLOR

The
Reinvention
of
Ivy Brown

Atlantic Books
LONDON

First published in trade paperback in Australia in 2008 by
Atlantic Books, an imprint of Grove Atlantic Ltd.

First published in hardback in Great Britain in 2009 by Atlantic Books.

This paperback edition published in Great Britain in 2009 by Atlantic Books.

1 2 3 4 5 6 7 8 9

A CIP catalogue record for this book is available from the British Library.

ISBN: 978 1 84354 775 4

Printed in Great Britain by Clays Ltd, St Ives plc

Atlantic Books
An imprint of Grove Atlantic Ltd
Ormond House
26–27 Boswell Street
London
WC1N 3JZ

www.atlantic-books.co.uk

For Winifred Roberts–Marney–James

The Reinvention *of* Ivy Brown

It would remain a black and white photograph in the spectators' and survivors' minds for most of their lives. Over time, the picture would get touched up and bleed into colour by those furthest from the blast, then embellished into their own personal drama.

Someone else's agony kidnapped by strangers as a piece of future entertainment.

Twenty or more onlookers stood on the spot, catatonic statues of horror. Their hands welded to their faces. From high above, office windows were thrown open and heads shoved out to scan the mayhem below. From streets away, everyone came to a halt, waiting for something more to occur. After the final boom came a steamy hiss and ooze of diesel, swirls of smoke, and the billowing of papers and city detritus blocking out the sunlight. Nothing else moved. Not a sound. Only the distant clip of heels trotting rhythmically through puddles somewhere along the street.

Ivy passed by on the other side of the road without a blink

at the disaster and turned right on to Southampton Row. Even here she had to chicane her way through a hushed avenue of paralysed traffic and people. The stolen umbrella, almost as high as herself, was tossed casually into the municipal bin on the corner.

After a few moments, her sole moving presence roused the street back to some kind of life. Strangers queried each other in whispers as to what could have happened and started to move en masse towards where Ivy had come from. Behind her she heard the ringing bells of ambulances and the fire brigade. Ahead of her, a bit of a jaunt away, was one of the main-line railway stations out of London: Euston.

Ivy wasn't dwelling on anything that had gone before. Instead, she followed the route embedded in her since birth. Once that door is shut, it's shut forever.

'You alright, madam?'

Outside the Boswell Hotel the lanky old doorman, in full blue and cream livery a few sizes too wide for him, was peering down at her. 'You look a bit dusty, were you caught up in whatever happened up there? Would you like to use our facilities? I'm sure that would be alright… in these circumstances.'

Ivy touched her hair and then her face in an act of delicate astonishment, and shook her head. She realized she looked absolutely filthy. Dust all over her two-piece costume, her handbag, and mud-spattered feet.

'That's very kind, thank you, I'm off to the station. I'll deal with myself there. Thank you.' She shook her little ginger head at him again, gave a grimace that was meant to be a warm smile, and clacked off down the street.

'Was anyone hurt, do you know?' he shouted after her.

Ivy, without breaking step, moved on.

She finally reached a stop point at the station. The trek had taken her forty minutes and it was now past five o'clock. At this time of day the Ladies Cloakroom was getting busy. Locked inside the cubicle, Ivy pulled the chain for clean water, soaked the handkerchief in the lavatory bowl, and wiped herself down from head to toe. Hearing the comings and goings of the female enemy outside, and what sounded like a queue forming, Ivy came out and finished her tarting up at the vanity shelf by the basins.

'The face that looks back at you from the mirror is never the same one you feel sure walks around the world with you, is it?' Two middle-aged women, plump as pigeons, had elbowed their way to the vanity area, powdering their noses, spit-licking bits of grey hair back into place and straightening coat collars and cuffs.

'I stopped looking close quarters at myself about twenty-five years ago, around the same time George did, which I regard as a blessing.'

Ivy couldn't get a toe-hold on these two classy frumps, taking up so much room in the tiny area, enjoying themselves and each other through their reflections.

'Poor eyesight and gas lighting kept my parents content for years. Absolutely no idea what the other looked like by the end. Violent lighting will do more harm in a marriage than any five-minute gasp with a young floozy.'

Squashed into a corner, Ivy patted her face with a new layer of pancake, put a slick of orange on her lips and attempted to push her frizzed-up hair into some kind of reasonable style. There was no need for powdering; the pancake was already beginning to flake as it dried. She couldn't get out of there quick enough.

Plonked in the Refreshment Room, as far away from the door as possible, Ivy sat with a cup of strong, sugary tea and read the posters and advertisements on the wall.

Night trains to Scotland... Night trains to Cornwall... Boat trains to France.

The clunk of metal on metal and the whooshing screech of brakes drowned out all the unwanted chit-chat going on behind. She thought how trains were never as romantic as they were made out to be.

Ten Pound Assisted Passage to Australia. The Land of Tomorrow. The poster was a very bright illustration of green fields and a cow.

PART ONE

Chapter One

1963 | FEBRUARY

Ivy stepped out of the lift and gave the commissionaire a conniving smile. Stopping inches away from the front desk, Ivy curved a saucy lean towards him as she struggled to put her mittens on.

'I'm sure you're snug as a bug in that marvellous creation, Mrs Brown, going out to lunch today, are we? Mind you don't slip.'

To anyone with an eye for these things, a small, sloping-shouldered, ginger-haired spinster in the brown black pelt of a beaver lamb coat didn't quite manage chic. Somehow the colour, the texture, and most of all the chunky weight of it, made Ivy's little head look like a Percy Dalton's peanut struggling to pass through the arse of a black Labrador. Head down, she pushed through the heavy double doors out into freezing air that razor-bladed over any exposed flesh.

The acquisition of this coat six weeks ago had put paid to any chance of cycling to work, quite apart from the ice age that had descended on the whole country the past two months. A

Christmas present to herself out of her fifty-pound yearly bonus. The best perk of working for an American company. The best coat that C&A Oxford Street had ever had in their shop. She'd go back to the bike in the spring, when the precious garment would be laid to rest in its special bag until next winter.

Ivy's mottled trotter feet warily tried to keep their bearings down the three icy steps, the inch-high stiletto heels of her plain black court shoes working as crampons to keep a grip. Her engine wasn't revving towards a sandwich. She was thinking about the weekend and Arthur. Where and how to slide into him by accident? They mustn't be seen together. By anyone. They could both lose their jobs for a start, and Arthur particularly had told her it was always a mistake to let people know your business. We are our own secret, he had said.

'We are our own secret.' Ivy knew that most likely he had got the line from the pictures, but enjoyed him mouthing it between kisses. It was as good as 'I love you' as far as she was concerned. She also knew he was right. If anyone got an inkling of their state of affairs and immoral yearnings, they could both be out of a job. Sacked for bringing scandal and gossip to the workplace. The heavier slur would, of course, be on Ivy: she, the older woman, an apparent widow, having it off with some young lad from the printers' depot.

Ivy went down the alley at the side of the building, hoping to find Arthur in the loading bay, slushing along the snow-covered cobblestones, making as much noise as possible but at the same time looking as if she had an important destination to somewhere other than him. She stopped and rummaged around in her handbag to have a chance to scan the backyard. The gates were wide open and she could see out of the corner

8

of her eye that the enormous snowman with a frozen stick of liquorice poking out of his mouth was still centre-stage, surrounded by three white Luderman's vans. He wasn't there. She hobbled on through the alley and out on to the main road of Kingsway.

Perched on a high stool, looking out of the window of Luigi's espresso bar, Ivy pondered her next move. She daydreamed the weekend with him, and the weekend without him.

Without him had the biggest picture.

Her mood couldn't rise to fun and warmth, only the hanging gloom of aloneness. She hadn't been able to get last night out of her head all morning. The tingling power she had felt when she discovered him waiting at the station, dangling keys and winking at her. How he had pushed her hand deep into his overcoat pocket to feel him at half mast, both knowing that they would have to be stealthy and walk the back alleys for at least another hour before the coast would be clear. Eventually the burglar sneak into the backyard, and a clamber up inside the back of the van. No words.

Under her coat, slowly moving up and down, Ivy dusted invisible crumbs from her right breast as she remembered his squeeze and bite through her brassiere; Arthur's knack to keep her frizzing and wanting. Long enough to finish the job, when her tangerine lizard lips swallowed him. Over the cartons of paper and brown envelopes, surprisingly, there was never any mess to speak of.

She allowed a tiny smirk to lift her face, thinking of his skinny limp back to Vauxhall that night, and what he might have got up to once he was home. The twenty-minute ride north to her bedsit in Islington had been a moist, warm rush to keep the fires burning. That last goodnight hot pee in the lavatory on the communal landing, and then back to the secrecy of her room. Stripped in a flash, clothes everywhere, Ivy jumped into the single bed and dived under the pile of blankets. Slow, muscular throbbings with the pillow pushed high between her legs. Many, many times she managed a pleasurable outcome. Nine she clocked up at the last count. Eventually, bored, tired, and suffering from leg cramps, she hauled her stiff limbs out of the little bed and carefully hung her costume and blouse ready for the morning to avoid any sign of crumpled habits and crumpled soul.

Jostling into her contemplations, a queue of half a dozen chilled bodies rattled out their individual lunch orders. For a moment she felt stark naked. Beneath the long shelf at the window was Luigi's only seating. Ivy sat at one end, as far away as possible from an old man further along. At first glance he could have been mistaken for a woman. The thick tartan headscarf tied primly, in royal fashion, at the point of his chin, was completely at odds with his ripped, greasy fawn raincoat and tar-covered boots.

Hunched and wrapped in the carapace of her fur coat, Ivy clamped her woolly mittens around the hot, frothy cup of milk. She had wolfed down the sandwich in four neurotic bites. A smear of margarine and a half-chewed knot were all that were left on the small white plate: the tail end of a sausage skin. Transfixed on the struggling traffic, Ivy stared out of the window: buses and lorries creeping along in the grit and filthy mush, hoping to avoid the hidden skiddy ice beneath. Great mounds of snow were piled high on the edge of pavements, showing no signs of piddling away yet.

Some larkers had rolled newspapers and stuck them in rows along the snow heaps, the papers freezing into a rampart.

She watched three young women come towards Luigi's, walking arm in arm and giggling, the blonde on the end holding out her engagement finger and then blowing on the diamond and rubbing it on her coat. The other two trying to get hold of her hand and pretending to take it off. A passing boy on a bike slow-pedals to a dawdle and gives them a wolf whistle. Shy shrieks that they may be making too much of a public scene, and they run out of Ivy's view.

A twinge of something unpleasant moves around her heart. She can't be sure if it's the girly friendship, the engagement ring, or the wolf whistle. Female company was not something Ivy lived for. She knew she was not a belonger, a safe confider. Mostly she was an avoider of women.

Every face that swept by the café was given the once-over, followed by a study of her own face reflected in the glass. She sipped her hot milk and her ribs grasped at something needling her: jawlines. She had looked at every woman with a jawline… and realized… hers had already gone.

Chapter Two

1963 | FEBRUARY

Janet Brady checked the backs of her legs. She was finishing her tea break, getting ready for her favourite part of the day: filing. Preparing for the architects' room first and all their sauciness, then downstairs to the 'Don't touch that yet I'm not finished' from some of the more poncy typists.

Although Wiseman Pulverizer used only the top two floors of this enormous marbled, curlicued building, everyone else benefited somewhat from the American company's extravagant twenty-four-hour heating. The main entrance on the ground floor had Mr Bertram at his commissionaire's desk and, opposite him, a busy Irish bank. Down in the basement was Luderman's, stationers and printers. Their entrance was through the backyard, where they kept the delivery vans, and they had an internal tradesman's stairway to the rest of the building.

The business traffic through the great front door constantly dispersed most of the luxurious warmth felt elsewhere, but it was better than nothing. At three o'clock in the afternoon the

Irish bank would close, and Mr Bertram could settle down to read, more or less uninterrupted, for the next two hours. The comings and goings would start up again when the office staff trundled out at the end of their day. The *Royal Air Force Flying Review* was Mr Bertram's close study, with its true stories of wartime heroes and escapades; other times he would scan *Dalton's Weekly* for second-hand puppets and any Punch and Judy equipment. *Airfix Magazine* would be saved for the Underground journey back to his two-room lodgings in Paddington.

Londoners were dropping dead from the smog and cold. Back in November, when the weather was beginning to get really bad, Wiseman's had issued face masks. By February around seven hundred people had choked their lives away in the putrid yellow poison. A handkerchief would return home after a day out black and sooted.

'Oi, I can see right up your skirt. Fancy milk and a dash after work?' Brian, Luderman's delivery bloke.

Janet looked down the stairwell into his amazing violet eyes and felt her face burn. Brian was so good-looking it made hearts over-pump the blood. He was more film-star dashing than Little Joe, her favourite, from *Bonanza*. But Little Joe didn't have that black glossy hair and those eyes.

'You delivering? Or have delivered? Bit late either way, isn't it?' Eileen Arthur, the tea-lady, was exiting the Ladies when she heard his voice. She put a protective arm around Janet, peered down the stairs at him. Like lightning he was gone.

'Why don't you like him?' Janet said.

'Did I ever say I didn't like him?' Eileen took a step back and searched around in the front pocket of her Wiseman's green overall; a plunge of Catholic guilt as Janet watched her fiddle with a blue and white gentleman's handkerchief. She couldn't find anything else to say, so mumbled a 'Sorry', having absolutely no idea what she was sorry for.

'What I don't like is him traipsing up here for no good reason. Well, I have a bloody good idea of his reason, but you're just a kid and he's a grown man. It's not right. If I told Miss Armstrong about him she could get him the sack, I reckon… and look at the time… The sack for me if I don't get a shift on.' Janet knew that Eileen had her own furtive whisperings with Brian sometimes, when she thought no one was about. There was no way she would get him the push.

Janet followed her along the corridor, back into the narrow kitchenette, and could see that the typing-pool tea trolley wasn't fully organized yet.

'Do the backs of my legs look alright? Normal?' Janet whispered.

Moving backwards and forwards, placing sugar, milk, and teaspoons in their place, Eileen glanced a couple of times the girl's slender legs.

'They seem perfectly alright to me, the stockings are a bit washed out looking, that's all. Why?'

'Nothing,' Janet said, readjusting her black velvet Alice band. It made Eileen smile that this pretty young girl should worry herself about a pair of legs that had everything going for them as far as she could see. But Janet wasn't fretting about the shape of her legs, she was fretting about the backs of them. Her day had cracked badly from the beginning.

There had been pandemonium that morning, the conductress having rows with all sorts on the top deck. Passengers were always a bit more frisky on a Friday, with pay day and the weekend off to look forward to. The top deck fugged up with Wild Woodbines being puffed, swearing and piss-taking of the fat conductress, then that terrifying helter-skelter on the ice when the bus went too fast around Old Street roundabout, with Janet almost obliterated as the stout conductress tilted and tipped on to her. As one, men in heavy boots had slammed and stamped their feet to aggravate the bus driver to be more careful. The comment that would eventually wobble the rest of Janet's day had only been half absorbed in the mayhem. It came as she swayed towards the stairs, ready to hop off at the next stop. Not a mention of was she alright, or a mind how you go.

'It looks deplorable, hasn't your mother passed comment? It wouldn't go amiss if you gave the backs of your legs a good wash, young lady,' the conductress boomed, making sure that all and sundry turned round.

Later on, Tony the crooning Italian newsagent put his two-pennyworth in. Not at first. At first he reminded her she was late.

'You cutting it fine, en't you, dharling?' He had pointed, without even turning round, to the clock behind and above his head. It was as she was running out, clutching her breakfast of a bar of Fruit & Nut, knowing that she was going to be at least ten minutes late for the first time in her life, that he called again.

'Eh, you bit of dirty gel, you no wash this morning?'

He'd pointed at her legs and swivelled his index finger. There they were, the marks of shame. The streets had not only marbled slush and mud on her nylons, but all the way through to her skin as well. And it didn't look like brand new dirt.

When Janet finally got to work she'd taken the lift instead of the stairs so that Mr Bertram didn't clock anything. Rolling down her stockings in the lavatory, with a bit of spit and rubbing she'd managed to disperse the grime into lighter swirls of grey. Had Brian noticed anything when he'd looked up her skirt?

'Come on, chop-chop, back to work, missy.' Eileen zigzagged the trolley past her. One last neck-crane at her legs, then Janet took a deep breath and quietly slid into the architects' office.

Chapter Three

Through the earpiece the Dictaphone droned on, Ivy's fingers on the keys following its demands:

Dear Mr Slack,
Re: our conversation of the 9th…

On top of having the audacity to venture out for lunch, then being five minutes late back, Miss Armstrong's gift of the evil eye had added to the inventory of Ivy's humiliations. It had taken the few seconds bothering herself before she noticed the date. Bashed it out like a robot.

Hanging there under the bold green (green for grass, she supposed) embossed company heading. Wiseman Pulverizer Company. The American company in London since 1951, designing heavy farm machinery for the rest of the world. They had also cornered the market in fertilizer.

Re our conversation of the 9th…

There was this bigger stain on the paper: 15th February 1963.

Her daughter's birthday. The fifteenth of February already. Her gallivanting with Arthur last night had scraped away the month, the year, the day of the week. Long forgotten, the dreaded, on-your-own New Year's Eve of six weeks ago. Then the other inevitable reminder. In roughly two and a half months' time it would be her own birthday. Her thirtieth. She detested these fanfare days where everyone pretends happy and smiley togetherness. The office world of cakes and cards to surprise the whichever birthday girl, who, to cap it all, is probably hated anyway. I can't be nearly thirty… I can't be this old. She tried a key shift in her mind, but it wouldn't go away. Thirty. The creepy-crawly slither to the grave, all options diminishing.

Her hands were plonked graveyard rigid over the keys and she could see her mother's hands. Well, not quite. Ivy's showed nothing of hard labour in the fields of Lincolnshire. Her hands were London-soft after ten years of city living, but the stunted broad clodhoppers hanging at the ends of her bony, freckled wrists were a dead giveaway of peasant genes.

Afternoon tea in a white porcelain cup and saucer, with dainty red roses painted round the rim, was placed by the side of her typewriter. Delivered by a hand so different from her own. Ivy was transfixed by this floating elegant hand.

'Slice of Victoria sponge to accompany that, Mrs Brown?' History hung in the air for a few seconds.

'Mm?' Ivy slipped off the earpiece and let it dangle round her neck. She had been working at Wiseman's for about four years and this woman had always been part of the building, as far as she could see. But she hadn't seen. She had never noticed anything about her before today. Today's hand. Today's date.

'Sorry… mm… no thank you… I went out and had a very full sandwich.' The tea lady moved off to the next line of cubbyholes. Ivy watched this body and trolley disappear into avenue four. Only her head was visible.

Five rows of five. The office had been designed in the American style. The typists had their own little private wraparound wall on two sides, covering their backs and the left-hand side. About four feet high, made of hardboard and painted green, with the company name printed on the back side of each wall, just in case anyone forgot who was paying their wages. Miss Armstrong would patrol this, her domain, every moment she could. After finishing her shorthand with Mr Jacobs, that is.

Miss Armstrong, a bony arrow of venom.

'Oh, Eileen, sorry but this cup is horribly cracked…' frothed the posh blonde on row four. 'Just have the tiniest sliver… no, less than that… else I'll never get into my frock, will I?' The posh Imogen who went skiing every year and was getting married in June to someone called Piers. Getting married and giving up work to look after him.

Eileen. The hand had a name. The face that Ivy had looked at today, properly, for the very first time. Looking into the face of someone at least ten years older than herself.

How come? Washing up all day long and having hands like that?

Banging away at the typewriter, hypnotically absorbing the words coming from the Dictaphone, she was dragged back to the date: dates, death, daughters. Ivy stretched her neck and opened her lungs to grab some air, trying to push away these evil, sticky cobwebs. Think of Arthur. Think of the lovely new coat. Remember the pillow, she told herself. Eileen, three rows down, was staring at her.

The fat girl with the constant blocked nose in cubicle two honked that she would like two pieces of that marvellous-looking sponge. Eileen delicately placed two slices on a saucer. Before moving off, she faced Ivy full on; an intimate slow shake of her head, three times. It felt creepy, as if they were familiars; some private behind-the-bike-shed sign. Ivy was flummoxed.

Chapter Four

1983 | LONDON

Another Sunday, another stiff kick at the gates of hell. The flower-seller outside the lodge of Mortlake cemetery had treated Eileen, once again, to an extra bunch for free. Six tall blue irises, with their sharp flash of white, had become twelve. Four graves to liven up.

Did he spoil her with these little gifts because she was a regular customer? Because he could tell that she lived on the bare necessities of a state pension? Whatever the reason, at sixty Eileen was not too proud to mind either way. They never consciously looked at each other. For twenty years, meeting every Sunday morning, here on the corner. He counted out his flowers, while she concentrated on the innards of her dun-coloured plastic purse with its little chrome clasp at the top.

Today had something different about it. The woman who worked the stall with him didn't huff a mood over the free flowers, as she usually did. An atmosphere of intimate boredom and irritation between the two flower-merchants reeked of a comfortless marriage. And that is what Eileen had taken it for.

Most graveyard visitors came around midday, just before their lunch, or last thing late afternoon. Eileen had always been one of the early birds. First thing Sunday morning, the hour-long journey of one bus, one Tube, and then another bus that dropped her off almost outside. Setting off on the dot of eight, to arrive at the latest nine thirty, her trip would be quietly uneventful. A safe distance from the dawn chorus of the first transport moochers. The prostitutes clocking off and ready to find breakfast, the fornicators and drunks trying to unravel their way home, and those other early Sunday morners, the impatient flea-market bargain hunters rummaging through the hawkers' confusions before they are even unpacked.

Four graves to tend in their individual ranking of love: 6-H, 10-V, 1-G, 10-Z. Eileen knew the plots by heart. She often passed the time, during her fitful Saturday night crumplings, and sometimes between buses, thinking about changing the order of visitations.

First on the list: the almost oldest grave. Mrs Clarke's posy would be delivered and placed with a sense of duty only, no tears, no mourning.

Two graves were relatively fresh. 1-G had been there three years now, and 10-V just over a year.

She would save the most precious, the oldest plot for the final leaving: 10-Z.

Eileen trudged along an avenue until she came to the H crossroads, old Mrs Clarke's final stop. None of the prized irises would ever be wasted here. For the past eighteen years the white plastic vase, Grecian-urn style, that was glued to the top of the headstone, had been filled every Sunday, come rain or shine with pungent herbs, grown on Eileen's kitchen windowsill for this very purpose. The living smell of the old woman, her diabetic sweats, the abscesses, entwined with the reek of the damp micey basement, had not gone to heaven with her, as far as Eileen could tell. Crouching down, she pulled out of her overcoat pocket a tiny roll of tinfoil which was keeping the few sprigs of thyme as sweet-smelling and long-lasting as possible.

Eileen had worked hard over the years to cremate any left-over ponderings, of who knew what, and the when and the why of it. But Mrs Clarke's foxy knowing grin would not burn, and sneered in the embers.

'I cleaned you up in life, and I'm still tidying and straightening you in death. For how much longer, eh? Who'll look after me when I'm gaga? When I start pissing myself and everything? You weren't that gaga though, were you?'

As she stretched at an angle to reach the urn, the thick socks inside her wellington boots couldn't prevent the hard, cold February ground from piercing through. Her arm wasn't quite long enough to stretch without a bit of a knee-press into the soil above the deceased. If she had gone from behind she would have been kneeling on a stranger, and Eileen didn't fancy that much either.

Instead of getting back on to the path, she meandered northwards through the graves, and then turned right into avenue ten. The very edge of the cemetery.

If anyone had been passing 10-v, and they weren't, they couldn't have heard Eileen mumbling into the green, crystal-covered plot, nor seen that her lips were barely moving, as she propped three irises against the little slab, swept off a couple of shitty pigeon feathers and some empty sweet papers.

'"Mum". Funny word, isn't it? "Keeping Mum." Well, we all did that alright. And you were the expert. Or maybe I was. Too late now. Irises. I know you were never keen, but I like them. Three for you and three for him. Don't really know why I bother with the flowers at all. Anyway, they're free, so nothing to fret about. Twenty years of silence and now this.'

She straightened up, brushed her coat, and didn't give an upward glance to the grave four sections beyond. That would be her final stop.

She now had to march across the whole width of the cemetery to get to dead person number three, 1-G. She was much more used to this one than the last, having been dealing with it for the last three years. There was no need for thoughts or words, just housekeeping of sorts.

This grave had a headstone that showed itself. The other two had been tiny little concrete things poking out of the soil. But here was a three-foot high, two-foot wide fine example of the stonemason's craft. If you wanted the history of the man, it was here in one line: 'Death Closes All'. Underneath, etched in what looked like gold, there was his date of birth and date of death.

One last look at the quotation and she said, 'I do hope so.'

Chapter Five

1963 | FEBRUARY

Shivering in the cold, waiting at the bus stop, Janet spotted Brian coming out of the shop with the evening paper. He was completely unaware of her. She had never seen him at long distance before. He had that funny little leg thing, which ever so lightly dragged. No, more kicked in front of him, as if to get moving properly. Her heart crashed against her ribs. Too shy to call out to him, Janet hopped around in the cold, hoping her movement would make him look across the road.

It was Tony who spotted her first. He had run out to give Brian something; some change, it looked like. 'Hey, you beautiful dirty gel, good day you have? Going home now?'

Brian turned round. His violet eyes twinkled over to her. Tony saw them look at each other and had to interfere. 'Yeah, she lovely gel... don't you mess her about or me duff you up, glamour boy.'

The backs of her legs came to her, and whether he would remember this morning and have fun with it. And what would someone as special as Brian think if he thought she was a dirty girl? Tony gave her a little salute, and chuckled off back to his shop.

Brian mouthed something, but the bus she was supposed to have got on roared away and drowned him out. He skipped that funny little skip of his and cantered across the main road. She screamed as a bus coming the other way missed him by inches.

'You fucking silly little bastard, why don't you look where you're going? I could have killed you.' The driver was livid, and looked white as a sheet.

'Keep your hair on … it's your unlucky day, you missed.' Brian was grinning as he hopped in front of the bus, gave the driver a little wave, and came over to her. She was embarrassed by the noise that had burst out, and now the bus passengers were stretching over each other to peer out at them.

'What are you doing tonight then my little post-girl?'

Janet looked around. The bus stop was empty. She studied her fingernails. Looked to the ground, at his snow-covered winkle-picker boots, then lifted her head, cheeks getting hotter, and braced herself to face him and those lovely brilliant eyes.

'Haven't decided yet. Bit too cold to meander, I reckon,' she mumbled.

He laughed a giggly, happy laugh.

'I'll tell you what, why don't I walk you to the next bus stop while you have a little think. If not tonight, what about tomorrow? Or Sunday?'

He put his arm around her shoulders and steered her on to the next stop. All sorts of peculiar things were happening in different parts of her body and, to keep this a secret from him, her shoulders and back went rigid and undeclared.

Although these friendly chat-ups had been going on since last summer, she was hooked now. The thought of having a boyfriend at all, never mind this particular one, was giddy-making.

None of this was easy-peasy; her mum and dad would give her the third degree if she let loose that she had a date or wasn't coming home until a bit later. Life was never as simple and free as this Brian probably imagined it was. Maybe Sunday afternoon was a possibility. She could wait until after dinner when dad went for a lie-down. She'd have to think of something really good, otherwise she would have to take Katherine with her, or, even worse, one of the littlies.

'Sunday. I could see you Sunday afternoon… for a walk or something.'

They had reached the next bus stop and so had the bus. Janet jumped on to the platform and, as she was the only passenger waiting, the bus was tinkled away before he could say anything. She ran up the stairs to the top and looked out of the back window. He was still there, doing a little dance, twisting away to Chubby Checker in his head. Then he blew her a kiss, just quick enough before the bus turned the corner.

He didn't know where she lived, she didn't know where he lived, so that was that until Monday. Or maybe he was just having a flirt with her. Maybe he was like this with all the girls. A great guitar twang of jealousy quivered across her chest.

The real Janet wanted to rush home and tell Mum all about him, but that could mess up her possibilities. Lots of questions, and then Mum might get Dad involved, for safety's sake? Would the rest of the kids find out and make fun of her? Big brother William must be seeing girls and all sorts, nobody asked him much. Working with Dad and being the eldest boy prob-ably put him wherever he wanted to be. But at this moment Janet was still a schoolgirl who just happened to be going out to work and making a wage. Nothing much in her life had changed since escaping St Edmund's Girls. There had been the boys from St Edmund's hanging around at lunchtime, but they were quickly shooed away and given dire warnings of hell by the nuns. Any good Catholic girl seen laughing with boys was given very short shrift for at least a week, and sarcastic comments from the Lord Himself could hit you in the eye even in the middle of a geography lesson. St Edmund's girls manip-ulated hard to avoid becoming the 'sniggered of the week'.

By the time she had got off the bus the February night had well and truly closed in. The ten-minute walk home, making slushy snowballs in the dark, gave her time to make up her mind. Brian wouldn't be mentioned yet. She would give it an-other week at work and see if he came on to her again. But. She could begin the freedom ticket.

'Janet? What happened? You're very late, young lady. We're all done, your tea is on top of the saucepan, now don't scald yourself.'

Before she had a chance to do anything, her mother grabbed her hands and started rubbing them between her own. 'Oh look at you, you're bloody freezing, and where are your mittens? Go on, take your coat off and I'll get the food.'

Her dad was asleep in the armchair, his feet almost in the grate. She could hear William in the bathroom, sluicing away, getting ready for his Friday night out. It was half past six and Janet should have been home half an hour ago. The two littlies, Mary and John, were hiding under the dining table, whispering and fighting over the potato men's plastic noses and ears. Katherine would be in the girls' bedroom, reading comics.

Janet moved her meat pudding into the bogs of gravy and tried to imagine an appetite. She couldn't swallow much, even with her mother giving her the beady eye. She knew she had to say something. 'I ran for my bus and I know the conductor saw me. Would he wait? I couldn't believe it, and it was freezing, Mum, so just to keep warm I walked to the bus stop further up and hoped I wouldn't miss the next one. I thought I'd never get home.'

Maureen gave her a hug and kiss on the cheek, told her to eat up while it was still hot, and got ready for the bedtime struggle with the littlies. Janet felt the tiny fib fall out so easily; a small shame brushed her.

The next few hours would follow the usual regime. Always an hour to get the littlies washed, into their nightclothes, a kiss for Mummy and Daddy, and then John off to the boy's room, Mary to the girls' room. Katherine reading or singing John to sleep, Janet doing the same with Mary. In their beds by eight o'clock and with a bit of luck both asleep by half past. Everyone but Maureen would be in bed by ten; she would wait, knitting, for young William to come home. If he dared come in after midnight… well, Dad would be got up, and the priest might even be informed.

'Night, Mum. Night, Dad. Oh, I wonder if it's alright if I took Katherine on a… well, an afternoon out on Sunday? After dinner? And we'd be back by teatime. She's sparko at the moment so she don't know anything about this yet.' Janet casually draped herself round the door, half in half out of the room.

'Sunday? In this weather? Where were you thinking of going? How far?'

'Just a bus ride, sort of, show her where I work. Then from there I could take her down to the Embankment and show her the boats.'

Silence, as imaginings of altered routines percolated through.

'Well, as long as you're back before dark. Alright?' her dad said.

'Smashing. Night night.' Janet contemplated giving them another goodnight kiss, but thought better of it.

Whenever she conjured him up, her take on a Mississippi accent came too. Last night he came to take her in his private plane to Acapulco, with yet another present. A light blue pillbox hat, identical to Jackie Kennedy's. But this night he would not come. She tossed and turned and could not conjure him up. In his place was Brian. Brian being nearly squashed by the bus. Brian looking up her skirt and twinkling with mischief.

Janet had had a long-running relationship with Elvis Presley. For about three years now she had looked forward to going to bed and reigniting the previous night's story. Elvis in love with her, Elvis searching for her. He rarely came to her during the day, and now he was fading from her life forever. Brian was in the leading role – she couldn't shift him. Eventually she fell asleep, the last billowing thoughts were what to do with Sunday.

Chapter Six

Ivy Brown's Friday night was just as topsy-turvy. Six thirty. She'd been sitting in the Rose and Crown for almost an hour. A woman sitting in a public house on her own could be mistaken for a bit of a hussy, however ladylike she sipped at her glass of Babycham, however posh her beaver lamb coat. Ivy pushed her cold trotters back into her shoes and braved another trip to the bar. It was warm and fuggy in here, with not too many men hanging about. She wasn't keen on the barmaid's sniffy manner, though. Awkwardly, both women negotiated the purchase of another Babycham and a packet of crisps.

She'd spotted Arthur talking to that young girl at the bus stop, nearly getting himself killed in the process. The girl looked like that little Miss Alice Band who worked at Wiseman's collecting the filing. He had never mentioned her, never said he knew her. Ivy had turned round and seen their reflections in the window of the electrical shop. She saw them head off down the road, with his arm around the young kid's shoulder. Gone from her eye-line, she had focused back on the irons, kettles and spin dryers that filled the window.

It was that scream and the skidding that had stopped the world for a few seconds. She felt cold and a tiny bit unwell. With feet turning blue inside brown pointy-toed shoes.

When little Miss Alice Band screamed… what had she called him?

The thought of hanging about in the freezing February cold had tugged against the misery of a lonely night in that little room in Islington. It was pay day. She was free to do anything she wanted. But she had no idea what she wanted, other than to be with Arthur, somewhere, anywhere.

'I'll have half a pint of brown ale if you're buying, Ivy.' The young man's arrival caused a small, guilty shift to come over the barmaid.

With their drinks, they moved to her table in the corner by the fire. Before settling down, Ivy half-turned her back, commanding Arthur with a lecherous twinkle to slip off her coat; letting him know she had well and truly warmed up.

'Bigger than you are, that thing,' he said. The most perfect line to make her feel petite and rather young. She giggled and tutted at him. They never did conversation as such, only little titbits to fracture the quiet. Here and there a nod, a smile, that was all.

'Thinking of staying here all night, or have you got other plans?' he carried on.

'Not really, I came in here to get warm and treat myself. I might get some fish and chips on my way home and have a quiet night in, listen to some music and that. If I can make the blooming aerial behave itself.'

32

'That sounds cosy, am I invited?'

He paid their fares on the two buses it took to get to Ivy's place. The journey time was filled with an embarrassed shyness, each waiting for the other to make some kind of intimate move. Not looking at each other. Not speaking.

The second they were off the bus, and away down a side street, Ivy let her hand accidently bang against the side of his thigh, ready for Arthur to grab and shove down deep into his trouser pocket to feel him getting ready.

The gas fire, the little bed and eiderdown would be a much more luxurious option than the van and the buff envelopes in this weather. But there was a problem with the landlady down in the basement that she would have to deal with. Assessing Arthur clinically, Ivy knew she had a pretty good chance of getting away with him if she blatantly owned up to Mrs Chircop that a young man would be in her room for a few hours. Not to worry about anything untoward, he was her little brother bringing news of a horrible family crisis.

Ivy was a quiet lover, giving little away. Arthur, dangerously more abandoned, was encouraged to bite on the bedding at the crucial moment.

The wireless was crackling with interference, not turned on loud enough for complaints, but enough to suffocate, hopefully, the flesh and muscle skirmishes playing out on the single bed. They had never had it so comfortable. Although it was done fully dressed, with only his relevant openings undone.

He came, he went; and Ivy was left again with her pillow for comfort. She was starving; the fish and chips had never happened. She stared at the ceiling, mobbish laughter coming from an audience crackling through the wireless. She felt a roaring purr go through her. He can't do without me, she reckoned. Arthur came back... no one can give him all I give him.

Warmed and self-satisfied, Ivy marched to the chippy, the cold night blasting her smeared face and lipstick.

The weekend was now full of hope. She made up her mind to discover Vauxhall. Go for a long A-to-Z nose round the area. All she had ever managed to winkle out of him was Vauxhall, when he'd trip over the details of the winter hikes to get to work. She needed to know and see where he lived. Get a few groceries, buy a magazine, perhaps find a little café; Ivy imagined being extremely continental and cityfied. And there would always be the edge that she could bump into him at any time.

If she didn't come across him and ended up being none the wiser, the second plan of action would be to walk across the bridge to the Tate Gallery, an elegant cultural afternoon with other elegant cultural customers... I might even take myself to that small picture house in the King's Road I've heard the snooty blonde 'who is going to marry Piers' talk about, she thought. In all these ten years I've never been to the King's Road. I'll leave the launderette until Sunday... or... no, maybe I should do Vauxhall on Sunday and the launderette tomorrow.

Chapter Seven

1963 | FEBRUARY

Part of it was working out quite well. Katherine didn't fancy strolling about in the cold, nor did the littlies. Everyone thought it was a bit too nippy for people with common sense to go a-wandering, especially when they didn't have to. After the Sunday roast, Katherine would scuttle the littlies round the corner to nan and grandad's for a few hours, while mum and dad could have a quiet snooze. If Janet was still determined to go for a jaunt on her own, then she could, once the washing up and everything else had been done and put away. That would give her about three hours to explore. She had to be back at six o'clock.

By Saturday night, Janet was thinking it might be a better idea if she went with someone.

The two school pals were leaning across the counter from one another. It was quiet, for now, only seven o'clock. By the time the Saturday night pubs chucked out, Susan Lee would be rushed off her feet, coping with drunk young men, starving and impatient for their Chinese takeaway.

'You don't open on a Sunday, do you?'

Susan and Janet had been inseparable at school, but now the grown-up world of work kept getting in the way of their past and present secrets. The nutty smells of rice and spices floated through this sterile square little shop. Strip lighting brutalized the brown and cream whirly-patterned tiles on the floor, and scruffy pine cladding on the walls didn't contribute anything more restful. There was a Chinese paper calendar, drawing-pinned to the wood near the half-glass door, and by the counter a wonky typed menu. Some bright plastic flowers sat in a Pyrex jug next to the till.

'You know we don't, nor Mondays either. Why?'

'I'm going for a bus ride tomorrow afternoon, on my own. No kids or anything. Fancy a little explore? About three?' Janet said this loud enough for the Lee parents to hear.

'What for?'

Janet peered through to the busy kitchen to check the coast was clear, then whispered, 'I might be seeing some bloke. Don't really want to be on my own.'

'No! What's he like? Where'd you meet him?' Susan's tiny moon face revealed hints of over-excitement. Not something that happened often. Their secret was interrupted by the arrival of the Bradys' supper, greaseproof brown paper bags full of fried rice, chicken chow mein, and two cardboard cartons of curry sauce. Delivered to the counter by old granny Lee, a thousand years old, who didn't speak any English. Apparently. Susan would never take a bet on how much the ancient one could decipher when she wanted to.

It wasn't going to happen. Susan's Sundays were spent with her grandmother, scrubbing out the fryers and shop floors ready for the following week. Mondays weren't any good either. That was cash-and-carry day. The girls' partnership was reduced to this regular Saturday night order for the Bradys. Susan worked nights and Janet worked days. Janet would have to ramble on her own.

'You still wanting to go out on your own tomorrow?' Maureen was helping with the washing-up.

'I'm not going on my own now. Susan Lee fancies a ride out. I mean, she never goes anywhere, does she?' This fell from her so truthfully that for a moment she believed herself.

The noise from the front room broke up any further possibilities of questioning. Young William, still suffering from last night's hangover, was getting belligerent with the littlies running riot before their bedtime. The more he hollered, the more they screeched just to aggravate him and manipulate Maureen into coming in and giving him an earful.

After his supper, young William and his Friday-night hangover would usually sit outside on the wall with his mates, bored and smoking, planning how to get to Southend when Easter finally arrived. Who had a Lambretta? Who would own one by then, to get them to the seaside in style? But not tonight, he felt too rough, and was going to get to bed as soon as the littlies were asleep.

Katherine was in the bedroom, learning, or pretending to learn, a chunk from the Bible ready for Sunday school the following morning. William Brady was next door at the McCreadys', playing cards. He wouldn't get home before eleven.

Up until this particular Saturday night, Janet had always

looked forward to these couple of hours on her own with her mother when the house was quiet before dad got back, mum knitting, chatting about the neighbours' comings and goings, while Janet played with the jigsaw on the sideboard. But she could feel an alteration in things these last six months. Her mother's voice had lost its story-telling edge. The jigsaw, a picture of a grisly band of cripples on their way to Lourdes, halos everywhere, now made her giggle at its awfulness. When she had first got it, two Easters ago, she had thought it the most heart-breaking and wonderful scene. Now she placed the top part of a calliper on to the wrong leg and burst out laughing. Maureen stopped in mid-flow of voice and fingers.

'No, no, it's not you, Mum, I've just made… I've… this picture is really hard,' Janet said with the giggles still filtering through.

Two white lies she had told in two days. Could this one be considered a third? She didn't feel the wrath of God. She would go to church with everyone in the morning just to be on the safe side, but no confession… not yet.

Janet kissed the LP with Elvis's glorious face, tucked it under the bed, and didn't say her prayers. Instead she scrambled under the pavement-cold sheets and dreamt of America and Him. Elvis did come to her in fragments, but mostly they were reruns, parts of stories she had been in before. These stories never got to endings, slumber would leave them in the ether, but tonight she tried to force a completion. It never happened.

Chapter Eight

1963 | FEBRUARY

Eileen pulled the plug out, ripped off the yellow rubber gloves, and picked up the tea towel. Round and round she wiped the saucepan, staring out of the window at the night. Tomorrow afternoon she would be back here, drying up the roasting things. Opposite she could see another woman, also at the sink. They were on nodding terms, but never while doing housework, only when colliding in public.

In the flat downstairs the only panorama would be of a brick wall three feet from the scullery window. Mr and Mrs Hodges kept a coop of pigeons out there for racing. Up here in Eileen's, although only one floor up, you could see the back-yards and behinds of the other houses. The two bedrooms above had even a better prospect, and her room looked over the street with all its comings and goings. Many a night would be spent peeping at the activities of the rest of the world, watching the girls leave the pub and wondering which one Brian would prefer. The girls having a laugh with young men nowhere near as handsome as him.

Albert and Rosa were now full-fed and comatose in the front room. It wouldn't be that long before they mooched into bed. Mantovani whimpering away on the radio was enough to send the liveliest to sleep. Eileen would stay in the domain of her sink until she heard their goodnight shufflings. She didn't know why quiet time to herself was the only way to manhandle her existence.

She supposed the war had made noise the enemy; a terrible time, living here by the river, waiting for all sorts of nightmares to occur. Wrapped up in a cuddly salmon-pink dressing gown in front of the coal-effect electric fire, dreaming into the make-believe flames, Eileen tried to imagine herself as the little girl before all that. She was sixteen when the war had started, but the sirens, bombs and horror had erased everything that had gone before.

Not much has changed in this house, she thought, furniture almost the same, the view almost the same. But the little girl that was me must have been some kind of lodger here. She's gone away. Not a ghost of her. Phantom life with human lungs to exhale a gentle breeze, not fire.

All that waste. Fleeting romances, one-night kisses, then the whoever boy back to the front lines before you could say Jack Robinson.

Ten o'clock. She could hear lively tinkles of laughter and music coming from the pub on the corner. The opening and closing of the door as the customers sozzled their way home. Maybe Brian wouldn't be too late tonight. She tried to unravel what he'd mentioned about his plans. The thing about Brian was that he could talk the hind legs off a donkey, turn this way and that, go off at tangents, and finally land somewhere entirely different from where he had started. He never actually said where he was going or what he was up to.

Whenever Albert and Rosa asked his whereabouts or what time he rolled in, Eileen would fabricate his life to them. The way she wanted his life to be; maybe the way she wanted her life to be. There were only eighteen years between the two of them, but he was brimming and bursting with life while she was slowly evaporating.

Her senses came round to the smell of fish and chips and the front of her legs scorching. Ten to eleven.

'Don't wake Mum and Dad up, Brian, stop clumping about.'

'Want a chip, Sis? Guess what? I won a fiver at the dogs. A fiver!'

'Shh… don't fib… there's not been any racing for months.'

'No… they've been on at White City for over a week. I just managed to catch the last two races. My dog might as well have had skis on, the speed he went… or she, I should say. "Eileen's Bridge", that's why I picked her. A fiver. Well done, old girl.' He dropped the greasy supper on to her lap and crouched over the fire, trying to warm all parts.

'Fancy going out like that, no wonder you're bloody freezing,' she said to his back.

The short jacket and drainpipe trousers in grey shiny mohair were too tight for anything warmer than a cotton shirt underneath. His weekend suit, made to measure for sixty pounds by a marvellous Maltese tailor off the Old Kent Road. It was what he'd wanted most of all for Christmas, and Eileen had got into debt for it. Brian had bought the black pointy ankle-boots himself. This outfit was his pride and joy.

Brian straightened up and took a handful of chips still

sweating in Eileen's lap. She gave his right leg the once-over and thought of that horrible time for the whole family.

'If Mum and Dad know you've been out like that... why didn't you wear your overcoat?' She broke her gaze with a nag, hoping he hadn't noticed her looking at his sore point.

'Don't tell them, then,' was his simple answer to everything.

'Oh, and don't make breakfast too early, will you?' he said going out the door. 'I want a bit of a lie-in.'

'Wakey, wakeeey! Come on, come and get it, you lucky campers.'

The lip-smacking fume of bacon frying brought Albert, Rosa and Eileen from their Sunday morning beds; that and the wireless blaring out band music. On the red-splattered Formica-topped table, Brian had laid out bread and butter, plates, tea in teapot, cups, everything, the *News of the World* folded and ready for Albert by his place.

'What's the celebration, he getting married or something?' Albert said.

Eileen's heart shortened and caught for a moment. The office, the girls, all jangled in and got mixed up with the morning. Brian married. Another generation of Mrs Arthurs. It would have to happen one day, she supposed. Please not yet. Please let me have some more time with him, more time here with us. It was the thought of not knowing her place in things, once he'd gone, that frightened her most.

'Where did you get all this then? Blimey, you've been up and about a while.' Rosa peered at all his organization.

'Mum, will you just sit down and eat, there you go.'

In relays – he could only fry a couple of eggs at a time – came bacon, eggs and tinned spaghetti for all of them. Finally he sat down to his own breakfast.

'You're washing up, Sis, I've done my bit.' Somehow Brian made everything sound bright and easy, like a magician who has brought the sun in.

'So, is it a girl, or have you robbed a bank?' Rosa asked.

'Believe it or not, this time it's neither. I won a fiver on the dogs!'

Chapter Nine

1963 | FEBRUARY

Ivy sat on the steps of the Tate Gallery and looked across the river. Ten o'clock Sunday morning. She had been able, for once, to enjoy the domestic chores of Saturday, knowing that she had this adventure to unravel today.

He lives somewhere over there. Probably still in bed if he's had a boozy night. She tried to imagine the home he lived in with his parents and sister. That's all she knew of him: Vauxhall, family. The view on the other side of the Thames was uglier and more industrial. Here and there she spotted some Victorian houses poking through the warehouses.

Ivy contemplated getting up and braving the gallery, but the sight of all the other visitors striding past her up the stairs, confidently chatting about the last time they had visited, made her feel like a criminal, rummaging through other people's luggage. She couldn't stay here on the steps, the bright high sunny morning did nothing to take away the biting cold. She could walk across the river to warm up or go inside.

The black woolly gloves held the collar of the beaver lamb

over her ears, but her freckled legs in thin stockings were beginning to change colour. I should have worn my bootees, she thought. Ivy had contemplated the bootees when she was getting ready, but just in case she accidentally bumped into Him, she wanted to look her best. The winkle-picker, sharply pointed stilettos did a not too bad job of disguising her plump little ankles and stumpy, size-three feet. The shoes also helped to elongate her from five foot one to an almost average five foot three, but the ginger bob didn't do Ivy any favours at all. Her fringe, which she had trimmed herself, was too heavy for her tiny sharp face. In the snow and damp her thick hair would have its own way and shrivel up into wiry curls. Which she hated: a plastic concertina rain hat was in her handbag at all times.

'You'll freeze there, honey.'

It made Ivy jump. She looked up into the face of... who?... what?

'Are you coming in or going out?' The elegant, deep, throaty voice didn't give anything yet.

As Ivy got to her feet, she noticed the black patent slippers, then stared at what was in front of her. Was it a man or a woman?

The apparition had short-cropped black hair above a wide, extremely pale, bony face. It was wearing a tailored black gentleman's evening suit of soft wool, white shirt with a grey satin tie. Ivy knew something wasn't quite right. It was the gash of red lipstick that threw everything out of kilter.

'Don't stare, darling, it's rude. Or did your mummy never teach you any manners?'

She was so posh, this 'thing' in front of her, the sound, the sureness, made Ivy feel diminished and unwashed. Smelling prey, the apparition took Ivy by the arm and ushered her into the gallery.

'Don't be frightened, I won't kill you. I just bite… a bit.'

The puzzle for Ivy was that nobody was taking any notice of them. Everyone else in the gallery was getting on with their own mumblings and shufflings around. There were some queer-looking people there. Young men with ripped cable-knit sweaters poking out from paint-spattered, scruffy duffel coats, girls with white-powdered faces, chalky lips, and thick black lines painted around their eyes. Most wore a uniform of complicated-looking bits of plush material draped around them, covered by dark cloaks with tassels.

She was manoeuvred away from the hall of dauby pictures into another, much quieter room. In here were more normal-looking, older types in their smart Sunday best, hushedly looking at large dark portraits of all sorts.

The grandest one caught Ivy's darting about eyes. Little yappy ginger and white dogs stood beside a great chestnut horse. A pretty lady in a pale-blue satin ball gown was beside the horse. Ivy noticed the small sloping shoulders and tiny, poached-egg breasts, just like her own, bobbing out of her cleavage. The room had about twelve pictures in it; grand ornate frames surrounding velvety rich people and their elab-orations.

'I love coming to this room, tipping the apple cart,' whispered the enigma. Ivy peered from under her curly ginger fringe and scanned the rest of the room. Almost as one, people began to vacate the room. A certain amount of pursed tight lips and blind eyes looking ahead showed on the faces. She couldn't think what to do for the best, so directed her gaze back towards the horse picture.

'Fancy lunch at the arts club? Then we can go back to mine, I only live round the corner. Oh, in case you feel the need to know, my name's Pandora... and please don't make the pun about the box.'

'Ivy. I'm Ivy.' Her voice had come out from somewhere at the back of her head. She had listened to this Pandora and didn't have a clue what she was on about.

'Ivy? Oh how marv! Do you cling?'

That hurt. She wasn't sure why, but it hurt.

The puppy demeanour was too much for Pandora. She grabbed Ivy by the back of the neck, stuck her hot tongue down her throat, slipped it back out, then closing her mouth, pushed a hard passionate frontal lip-to-lip kiss on her.

They stared at each other for eternal seconds.

'Do they have facilities in here... a toilet?'

Pandora pointed to a sign and said in a bored yawn, 'Daren't come with, I'm afraid.'

On the way to the lavatory, Ivy saw a different sign. Way Out.

Blown by a biting wind across Vauxhall Bridge, Ivy thought she must have fantasized the past lunatic half-hour. She was desperate to find somewhere warm and have a cup of tea or something. The sheer swank of Pandora and her kiss had stirred Ivy into a foreign empire. She had no language for it. It was men she understood. Or thought she did.

Over the bridge, Ivy traipsed along South Lambeth Road, to discover the only signs of life were a newsagent's and a tiny church emptying itself of women and small children. She bought herself a newspaper, ten cigarettes and a packet of

Rollos. As she was paying, she glanced in the slice of mirror between the cigarette shelves. Her orange lipstick had been smeared this way and that, mingled with Pandora's outrageous red.

She walked streets and streets of identical sleepy terraces, occasionally coming across once magnificent squares, now all dilapidated and slummy. Hardly seeing a soul, Ivy knew that finding a café here at all, let alone on a Sunday morning, was not going to happen. There were a group of men waiting on the kerb for a pub to open up, but she didn't fancy a sit-down enough to join the queue, today of all days.

She spotted a bus heading for Victoria station. Four people were hopping off in different directions as she was trying to board. She heard one of them say 'Hello' and then they were gone, the bus pulling quickly away. Ivy marched down to the front to get to the warm spot away from the open platform. Out of the window she saw a woman wave at her. A woman she did and didn't know.

Chapter Ten

1963 | FEBRUARY

Eileen had her own key to let herself in. There was always a moment, that catch of something. She had been expecting it much more this arctic winter. She prayed that it wouldn't be her bad luck to find and have to deal with it.

'Hiya, it's only me.'

Clenching the heavy suitcase full of ironing, she hovered with all senses as alert as she could muster. Wearing so many clothes muffled everything and kept the sharpness of the world at arm's length.

'Hallooo.' Her ungrounded voice floated down the dark silent hallway. The sweet mingled stench of mice, damp and sweat; diabetic sweat managing to permeate the freezing cold basement. In the summer it consumed everything.

'You're early this morning, Eileen.' Under the woolly tartan headscarf Eileen's scalp tingled with a fresh rush of blood. She peered into the gloom of the long narrow passage and saw old Mrs Clarke leaning heavily on her two walking sticks, trying to gesture with a flip of her fingers.

'Not had a winter like this for about ten years now, I didn't expect you to brave it today, if I'm honest. Lovely to see someone though, and I've just made a brew.' The old woman hobbled expertly on her sticks back into the scullery. The gas oven was on with its door open to warm and steam up the room.

It wasn't that Mrs Clarke was grubby, but her infirmity made it tricky to keep the place sanitary. Her sight was going, which made matters more 'how's your father' where cups and saucers were concerned. Eileen tried not to have too many imaginings as she sipped the tea, praying that the boiling water had slaughtered most things.

'So, how have you been, Mrs Clarke? Everything alright?'

'Not bad, Eileen, not bad. The nurse comes every morning, as you know; well, I say every morning, she couldn't get here last Wednesday because of the weather. Diabolical, wasn't it? The council people have been driving me mad to get out. They only want to put me in that bloody tower block on the Wandsworth Road. I'm not having that.'

'They're very smart, apparently; got heating and bathrooms and everything. I'd love one, but Mum and Dad are not interested, they don't want to move either,' Eileen told her.

'It's too much at our age anyway, moving. I'm not getting much sleep lately… got this terrible abscess at the top of my leg. Murder it is. From me injections.'

Mrs Clarke had managed to dress herself this morning, or she'd been sweating in the same clobber for days. She wore a knitted woolly hat over her thin grey hair, a matching scarf to keep her neck warm, and a long heavy black skirt peeped out from under her herringbone overcoat. It felt colder in the basement than in the February horror outside blasting everyone's cheeks off. Fingerless mittens couldn't keep the old girl's hands warm enough to stop the ends of her fingers turning a pinky-bluey tinge.

Eileen had watched Mrs Clarke deteriorate badly over the past two years. The diabetes had made her eyesight weak and her legs and feet even worse. Then the constant eruptions of abscesses where the injections went, and now she had another one. Too many layers of clothing had fortunately prevented any attempt at displaying the infection this time.

Sitting there drinking her tea and keeping one eye on the clock, Eileen's mind raced back to that Sunday last summer. Please, never again, she thought. The abscess had erupted in the heat of the bed during the night and Ada Clarke had been sweating with relief, the terrible pain finally exploding out of her. The mess had been savage. Cleaning her up was bad enough... having to fill the abscess hole with a tiny piece of lint drenched in antiseptic. But it was the touching and manhandling of the sheets, the carrying them in her suitcase on the bus, the washing of them in the public bathhouse, where everyone knew her, that had been the most hideous. She hadn't been that sure it was legal to wash such poison in a public utility.

The rank smell of those sheets had had to sit in Eileen's flat until the following Monday afternoon after work, in the stinking heat of summer, with Brian asking if she had a dead body in the case. She couldn't bring herself to tell him any part of the story. Knowing him, he wouldn't come near her for weeks, and that would break her heart. But for days after, she carbolicked herself skinless. The innards of the suitcase was showered in cat litter to break down anything lingering there, and then scrubbed and sterilized.

'How's that saucy brother of yours doing? Married yet?' For a flicker she thought the old girl must be talking about Freddy, blown to bits twenty years before in Tripoli.

Eileen found herself staring at the floor and then at Ada's legs. The baggy, washed-out long johns... and her husband had been dead a good twenty years... had a pair of old army socks over them, and the whole lot was crammed into a wide pair of hairy carpet slippers.

'Your Brian? He alright?' Eileen thought she caught a glimpse of something not that kind in Ada Clarke's foggy eyes.

'He won a fiver on the dogs last night and treated us all to a big fry-up with his winnings. Look at the time, I've got to get moving, Mrs Clarke, there's a joint of lamb needs seeing to. Mum'll have my guts for garters. She said she'll be round to see you as soon as the weather calms down.' Eileen couldn't wait to get out of the steamed-up scullery and away from the old woman's beady eyes.

'Oh. Don't forget your money. You know where it is. You've not unpacked yet, have you time to do that and put it in the bedroom for me, please?'

She put the clean sheets, pillowcases and two towels on top of the chest of drawers in the morgue of a bedroom.

'See you later.' And with that Eileen found herself in the snow and slush waiting for the number two bus. She had left in such a scurrying state that she had forgotten to strip the bed and take the dirty towel off the back of the chair, and now here she was with a completely empty suitcase. But she couldn't go back, not today. She wished that she had unpeeled at least some corners of her clothing while she was sitting in the scullery. The icy wind penetrated right through everything.

Through the black suedette bootees, heavy belted grey coat, muffler, headscarf, woolly gloves. Her open-to-the-elements legs and face felt wire-brushed by the wind.

'My brother Brian,' her nerves rattled, over and over again.

The weather pricked her eyeballs and tears cauterized her cheeks. It was a quarter to midday already. Dinner was always on the table by two; she would just about manage it, home was only four bus stops away.

And now another strangeness. As Eileen was getting herself down the stairs she could see a few people queuing to get on to the platform. And there she was. They almost came eye to eye. Ginger Nuts. But Ginger Nuts didn't recognize her. Not here, out of her apron and trolley. Jealousy powered Eileen's nerves, and as the bus gently pulled away she gave Ginger Nuts a little cocky wave. That'll fox her.

'My brother Brian,' ringing in her ears.

Eileen needed to get home, to get warm, but something bigger and icier than this February could throw at her called her to calm herself before she faced anyone. She crunched through the snow-clogged grass of Vauxhall Gardens into the empty playground. In an attempt to keep her coat and bum dry she put the empty suitcase on the seat of the swing and plonked herself on top. Impelling her legs hard to and fro, with head and shoulders arrowed fiercely against the air, she worked herself up into a high pendulum. Swinging backwards and forwards she tried to unravel the harm, the hurt. Brian. She would have to keep an eye on Ginger Nuts. What was Miss Fur Coat and No Knickers doing round these parts anyway... on a Sunday at that? With her tiny head poking through the pelt of her collar like a newborn terrier.

Brian. So, so handsome with his disobedient leg.

Brian with his sauce and laughter, his…

He's mine. He's always been mine. This banged against her head and she could find no way to organize it. Brian was also skirting and sniffing around the post-girl. Eileen wasn't over-worried about that. Little Janet Brady would be too Catholic, young, and awkward to let hot things boil into trouble. Eileen was pretty sure of that.

Finally, all the thinking and fretting in the world mulched back down to what she had always felt, would forever feel about him: 'He is the capital of my one and only universe.'

How to be the capital of his was Eileen's millstone.

'You'll never guess who I saw as I was getting off the bus… that Ginger Nuts from the typing pool at work.'

Eileen's occupied time in the kitchen, talking with Rosa about old Mrs Clarke, the forgotten dirty linen, the calming chit-chat of nothingness, had managed to focus her slightly better than time in the park.

'The who?' Brian's mouth, full of potato, squelched out the question.

'Oo, Eileen, this is a bit bloody, bit too bloody for me, do you mind if I swap with you, Brian? Look, she's given you the knobby end and the crusty bits.' Rosa exchanged plates.

'Mum! Do you want the spud back out of my mouth as well?' He gave his dad and sister a sparkling wink.

And it was lost. The weeny moment to surprise Brian into showing himself. Ginger Nuts would have to wait for another hard-worked-at, throwaway moment.

Chapter Eleven

1963 | FEBRUARY

Because Maureen had waved her off from the kitchen window, Janet was obliged to go the long way round, as if she was going to pick up Susan Lee. This took her on to Whitechapel Road, not the street to pick up the bus she was planning on. Maybe I'll go another route, she thought. I don't have a hope of seeing Brian anyway, do I? Twenty minutes she stayed upstairs in the mild air of this unacquainted bus. She saw St Paul's Cathedral's back end, where normally on her way to work she could see more of the side, saw bits of the Thames to her left, down Fleet Street, the Strand, and finally this is where she decided to get off. Trafalgar Square. Three thirty and already the light was beginning to go.

Janet walked round and round the square, pigeons running like rats after the few stragglers who had brought bread-crumbs. Bird shit everywhere. Fountains trickling miserably, as if they were too cold to be bothered displaying themselves. She noticed groups of young people sitting on the walls in front of the portrait gallery, St Paul's all over again it looked like to her.

She found a bit of wall between a youngish man on her left scribbling into an exercise book and on the right, a boy and girl kissing, nuzzling, and then kissing again. All around her, sitting on the walls, leaning against the building's pillars, crouching on the patch of grass behind, were these creatures. She had read about them in the *Daily Mirror*, heard about them on the wireless, knew what they were, but had never come across any in real life: beatniks.

Nobody took any notice of her, sitting there, listening to the sounds of freedom. Janet wondered where they got these strange outfits. How many years it must have taken to grow hair that long, or what it was that made others have it all chopped off into a little cap. Swirly skirts, black ballerina slippers, long scarves, and some of them even wore hats. They jingle-jangled as they moved around, silver hoop earrings, armfuls of bangles in silver or beads. Most of the boys wore black, heavy-framed glasses, huge ribbed jumpers with the elbows ripped, over skintight trousers and boots without lace-holes: smooth black boots with elastic sides. A lot of them had scraggly tufty bits of beard and floppy hair.

A picture of marching students, marching for something or other, she'd seen people exactly like this in the papers. I want to be one of them. I want to be a student, wearing anything you like, moving around your own life without grown-ups.

It was getting colder and darker, and not a clue as to whether she had been away from home hours or minutes.

'Have you got the time?' she asked the tufty-bearded bloke next to her.

'If you've got the inclina… oh, so sorry, too young for me. It's, er, quarter past four.' He showed her his watch and smiled.

Janet was trying to work out what he had meant to say when a flurry of movement from his group, about ten of them, disturbed the moment. 'We're all mooching off to Yvonne's, coming?' boomed a deep lah-di-dah voice from behind her.

'Who's Yvonne?' two girls chorused.

'You know. Yvonne. Gets fucked by her father.'

The crowd laughed and whooped with each other, then, as if a sheepdog had rounded them up, ran off together in a moving clump, some walking backwards, talking to the gang behind.

Chapter Twelve

1983 | HOLLAND

Flat, so flat. The far-away sentries of poplars have an uninterrupted view of me at the kitchen sink. And it's raining
again. I know I should get my hands out of the suds and bring
the bike out of the wet into the hall. But fuck it, I want to stay
here, scrubbing at the crutch of his underpants.

Please don't come home, not yet. I want this day to myself
and not have to speak, say anything. Don't come in and tell me
about the market, the traffic, how it's not been worth the aggra-
vation, how we will have to be careful for a while. I have
nothing in my mouth to shape out to you.

I'll sing, that's what I'll do. I'll sing an old school hymn to get
words and breath out of my head and into this kitchen… Into.
Fuck it, I'll bring the bike in.

'What do you want if you don't want money? What do you
want if you don't want love?'

Adam Faith. Christ, why that?

'What do you want if you don't want money? What do you
want if you don't want love?' I can't even get beyond two

frigging lines. I'm sure I used to know it all. Brian used to sing it, whistle it all the time.

Now the phone. I won't answer it. What if it's an accident? Answer it. If he died what would I do out here all on my own? Answer it. Suds and rain and mud all over my skirt now. Leave the fucking bike where it is!

'Ja? Met Mevrouw Vroegindewij... Oh, it's you... No, of course, you do that, I have lots to... Six-ish?... Okay, okay, you do that... Yes, see you later, bye.'

Another eight hours of staring into the back of my head. And why does he always have to speak English to me when he is on the phone and with other people? And loud, as if I'm an imbecile? First I want him to stay away, and now I want him home.

'Ik begrijp het als je langzamer spreekt...' This tongue can let me be a me. A charming, innocent, struggling me. I even charm myself with it sometimes. It's just dawned on me, I'm only a misery guts in English.

There's no dreaming in Dutch any more. Half a year, dreaming, thinking, has all been back to English. I've started to say 'Good morning' to the postman when for twenty years he has known me to greet him with a coy, sweet, 'Goede morgen, Mynheer Rovers.'

Would children have made some difference? Little Dutch children having a foreign mummy?

It can't be a hormonal day, can it? This has been a crawling, six-month torpor back into London-speak. Could the menopause start at thirty-six? Could this... these scratchings and peckings, be because I am drying up and turning back into what I once was? It wasn't a pleasant thing that happened that

Friday. But, Jesus Christ, it was twenty years ago. Something you read about in the papers all the bloody time. It happens to a lot of people. City life, it's what happens every day somewhere. Even here, out in the flat dykey sticks of Sneek, it happens. Sneek. I schneaked away to Sneek. How fucking appropriate.

Chapter Thirteen

1963 | FEBRUARY

Brian fingered the silver St Christopher. Patron saint of travellers, she had told him. He didn't want her spending money on him. All these little gifts, these sweet nothings, were beginning to take the shape of somethings. Propped up on one elbow, stretched out on his narrow bed, he stared into the flickering burner of the paraffin heater.

'It's a St Christopher and when I saw it I knew I had to get it for you. With all the driving around you do and that, it's to protect you from, well, ambush and kidnap originally, murder as well in biblical times. I read it in *The Lady*.'

It should have been a gentle thing, a kind gesture mixed with a bit of a laugh. A silver disc with a man and his staff, hanging from a short chain; the night-hag's lucky charm. When Ivy had locked it around his neck, deep in his boots Brian had felt ambushed and kidnapped already.

He pondered on whether to 'lose' St Christopher to Eileen. Make believe *he* had bought it for *her*. There was a devil's pong to that, some superstitious odour hanging over the idea. The last thing in the world he wanted was for anything to ever happen to Eileen.

Brian knew that he was supposed to reciprocate with a like-minded offering. Under normal circumstances that is exactly what he would have wanted to do. But he was beginning to feel that this experience with Ivy would never reach normal circumstances.

When she had presented it to him, all bushbaby fluffiness, that night in the back of the post-van, she had asked something very special of him. Well, she had called it 'very special'. Now he wasn't so sure. Ivy seemed to find the cheapest weakness in a man, that would turn itself into a schoolboy shame the next day, or the day after, or the day after that. Lying there, as he tried so hard not to resurrect it, the great smudge of the incident forced its way in. He blushed in his own privacy.

She had been kneeling in the back of the van, her hands in her pockets. In the darkness he'd sucked hard on her breasts, tasting the wool of her jumper and the rigid corsetry and nylon lace of her brassiere through that. Then she spoke and almost broke his moment, 'I've got a present for you.'

Their game had changed. It felt so exciting when she asked him to do it, and he did: to masturbate over St Christopher, as she held it in her palms. When it was done with she rubbed everything all over and through the silver chain and disc, then put it around his neck. What had she said? 'Every time you put this on you will think of me.'

The minute he was out of her sight he yanked it off. On the Tube home he owned up to himself that maybe it had been exciting, but, for all that, the afterwards wasn't good enough.

Brian thought of all his choices, how to pass the gruesome

mascot on: Fred at work; his mum; or carelessly lose it on the Tube, a bus. None of this sat right with him. Bad stuff. That's what St Christopher had become and he didn't want to pass it on to anyone. He felt girlish and silly in his voodoo imaginings. For safety's sake, it would stay in the sock drawer.

The knock on the door snapped him back into Vauxhall, his bed, his heater. Eileen didn't wait for permission, she walked straight in and went over to his chest of drawers, sitting under the window. His ironing for the week: three white cotton shirts, four white vests, and four pairs of green paisley-patterned underpants. A few pairs of brown socks were rolled up into balls. All a little biography of his habits. These were his work clothes; today's laundry had nothing to do with his weekend clothes.

Shirt changed every other day, vest changed almost every day, along with socks, underpants changed every day except Fridays. He never wore underpants on a Friday. It was just something that had become a habit since secondary school. In those days he was supposed to make a fresh pair of underpants last for two days, and that way they would last the whole week; but since Brian had been about thirteen and began the teenage fiddling with himself on a more regular basis, he liked to have clean pants on every day, so by Fridays he had run out of them. It never occurred to Eileen, Rosa, or even himself to buy a few more. More would be bought only when togs finally fell apart.

He watched as Eileen quietly put his things into the drawers, lastly dropping the socks into the small top drawer that also housed his motorbike magazines. It dawned on him in that split second that St Christopher couldn't be left to fester there.

'You alright, Bri? You were full of the joys of spring this morning…' He was staring at her. He wanted to be surrounded by her arms, be that little boy again, with her kissing the top of his head and telling him that by tomorrow life would be fine and dandy. Dread, or embarrassment, kept him on the bed.

'No, I'm alright, I was just thinking about your style. You know, you never dress up or want something smart and that… I look at clothes all the time.'

'One day you won't,' she said. 'One day you'll wake up and realize that you haven't thought that much about the outside of yourself in quite a while.'

His forehead had turned into a question mark. Brian searched for the outside of himself several times a day. To the extent of angling the mirror to examine the back of his head, the back of his legs.

Eileen stared out at the snow and slush for a few seconds, and then said to him, with a soft chuckle, 'Growing up is an interesting thing. I know much more about your growing up than my own, of course. I can look at you and remember all sorts, the first time you did this or the first time you said that, but I can't remember much at all about myself. As if Mum bought me in a shop somewhere when I was already sixteen. Maybe the war blew out unimportant brain matter, anything that was not worth the thought it was sitting on or something. Mm, I think it probably happens to all of us eventually, you open different eyes one day and have forgotten what it ever felt like to have people give you the once-over, and then you forget to notice yourself as well.' She gave him a gentle laugh and raised her eyebrows to heaven in some kind of apology.

Eileen could see him imagining this happening to himself

64

at some point. 'Some people are doers and some people are observers. I don't see how you can have the time to be both, frankly,' she told him.

'I don't think you miss a trick,' Brian said. He smiled with innocence; she smiled with secrets.

As she was leaving, Eileen popped her head round the door, 'Did you hear me at dinner? I spotted that Ginger Nuts from the office. She got on the bus as I was getting off. She don't live round here, does she?'

St Christopher cut into his fist. 'Who do you mean?'

Eileen had tried to sound any old how, but his question tightened her. He was avoiding something. She closed his door and he heard her shout down the passage, 'All fur coat and no knickers, that one.'

A horror map of what may have happened that Sunday afternoon was of Ivy Brown lurking in doorways, following and watching his every move. The bigger nightmare: his sister knowing what he did in the back of the van, what he'd done in Ivy's room. St Christopher, the patron saint of travellers, had to go. He hung the chain on a wire coat-hanger. Getting the medallion as close as he could, he dangled it over the paraffin heater. He thought if he could just disfigure it enough, he could chuck it anywhere and no one in the world would give it a second glance.

Brian gave up after about fifteen minutes, bored and hot, and dropped the coat-hanger on to a speedway magazine on the floor. The thing immediately scorched the paper and he had to quickly scrunch it all up. He could feel the metallic heat through half a dozen or so pages. His nerves were aggravated. I'm making a mountain out of a molehill. Why don't I just give her the fucking thing back tomorrow and tell her to stop following me? Another thought was to write her a note.

He ripped opened the toasted magazine and found that, although the chain and disc of St Christopher looked intact, on closer inspection the saint and his staff had melted into sludge.

Melted away. That's what must happen with this Ivy business.

Chapter Fourteen

1963 | February

Down in Aldgate, the snow, ice and slush had been getting on everybody's nerves since Christmas: each day more stories of old Mr So-and-so coming a right nasty cropper, buses at full capacity spinning out of control round Gardiner's Corner, it being too dodgy to ride a bike anywhere.

But up west people had a carnival feel to them as they slid and skated their way along the Strand. Twinkling brightness floodlit the pavements, giving the late-afternoon winter gloom a bit longer to make its mark.

These people Janet had snooped on and examined from a near distance didn't feel that much older than herself. Yet they were free to come and go as they liked. No time limit for them to get home; make it up as you go along kind of thing. Her bat ears tuning in and sucking up the rise and fall of their crossfire conversations; the one thing that kept filtering through was 'the Easter march'.

Janet followed the gang, not quite sure where it was going, but knew that pretty soon, to keep herself out of trouble, she would have to find a bus to get her home. Eventually they all stopped outside the Waldorf Hotel, inches away from the heavily brocaded doorman, and fell into a whispering huddle. She carried on past them a few yards and loitered around a bus stop.

They emptied their pockets and handed everything to the tall skinny student with the blond straggly hair and baby-fluff chin. Whatever the collection was meant for, it wasn't going to be spent in the Waldorf. The stout doorman, puffed up and proud in full rigging, blocked the access to the hotel's revolving door.

'Have you any idea who I am?' trumpeted a beautiful dark-eyed girl in black.

Snorts and boos all round.

'No one, whoever they think they are, miss, can come into the Waldorf Hotel dressed like that. Now, if you would please like to move along.'

Janet watched as the girl pushed into the doorman's face, as though to kiss him, and sounding just like the Queen, said, 'Bollocks to you, Your Lowliness.' On 'Lowliness' she gave him a deep curtsy. Janet was stunned by the whole performance. To sound like the Queen and say 'Bollocks' so sweetly was awe-inspiring. It was water off a duck's back to the doorman.

A bus bent gingerly around the corner into Aldwych, a number fifteen. She couldn't believe her luck: one damp, warmish bus, almost to her front door. She ran up the stairs as fast as she could to get one last glimpse of the little gang. The black-eyed beauty was running away from the group towards the retreating bus, shouting something, a name.

Janet ducked down a little from the back window, but kept a peeped eye on the street as the Waldorf disappeared.

'You watch and follow ush, yesh?'

It made her jump, this lisping, foreign, out-of-breath voice. Tall skinny blond with the long hair, wispy chin fluff, and smiley blue eyes. 'Brr, very cold these times. Don't you think so? May I have some room to sit with you for a while?'

She didn't have a clue what else to do, so nodded and sat herself down. Her cold nose was beginning to heat into a flame and she prayed for no embarrassing drippage.

'My name is Ben and I have watched you watching us for a long time. Did you see me watching?'

Instead of finding a reply, Janet began searching for her bus fare. She could hear the stomp of the conductor hauling himself resentfully up the stairs. They were the only two people on the upper deck.

'To Aldgate, please.'

'And for me also,' Ben said, handing out the fare for both of them and pushing her hand back towards her purse. He had given the conductor a ten-shilling note.

'Oh, for gawd's sake, haven't you got anything smaller?'

'Is this not a... what you call it? Legal tender?' Ben asked.

Both men stared at each other, Ben smiling, the conductor definitely not. Eventually he went back downstairs with an 'Oh, sod it.'

'It almost always works,' Ben whispered to her. 'Except when they are doing the last bus before the garage, then they like the big notes. Easy, you see, to count the money.'

'You don't live in Aldgate, do you?' Janet said.

'No, no. I live... Well, at the moment I live on the floor of a friend of my uncle, in Kensington, but soon I will find a room of my own. It's an antique shop, and I believe I am the burglar alarm. The just-in-case burglar alarm.'

The rest of the twenty-minute journey was spent with alien Ben talking solo. Her burning nose quietened down and she sank into the ramblings of his world: art school, Amsterdam, antiques, music; he'd even been to America. Elvis popped into her head for a second and flew out again. Brian took his place. Brian. The whole purpose of her day's adventure. And now this.

Art students were an unfamiliar sight around the back streets of the East End of London. In these parts, boys were schoolboys and then they were men, working men. There was no halfway house to grown-up time. Ben's brightly striped long muffler and grey duffel coat, skinny black trousers and scuffed boots, marked him as a foreigner. He hadn't acquired the working man's swagger to fend off any potential marauders either. That funny loping gait of protection, the strut of 'my balls are too wide for my hips' kind of thing. He walked gently, with his head slightly cocked to one side. Smiling and nodding as he talked, as if always agreeing with his own new thoughts. Janet called on her part-time God, to thank Him for the now dark streets, and to save her from having to confront anyone familiar to her. She squinnied up at Laski's the jewellers over-hanging clock: ten to six.

'I have to go home now. I go that way.' She was two streets away from the truth.

'I walk you to your home. It's too dark for you,' Ben said.

'You can't, you can't, my brother will hit you…. Well… more than likely.' The sudden rush for home, and her head spinning with a weekend of lying, stumbled and tripped all her thoughts.

'Okay, okay. Calm yourself. Can I see you again? I would like that.'

He dug out from the depths of his coat pocket a half-chewed pencil and some leaflets, and with arctic-numbed fingers wrote his name and a telephone number on one of them and pushed it into her hand, then lifting her chin, he kissed her cold nose. Janet stared, almost cross-eyed, into the blur of his hairline.

After a fleck of a moment, she was off down the street, sloshing and tottering through the mush, leaving him on the corner, quivering in the frosty air.

Janet weaved an excited tale of her afternoon adventure, relentlessly mentioning 'Susan Lee thought this' and 'Susan Lee said that', on and on, following her mother into each room. Six o'clock had been the perfect time to get home. Everyone was trying to organize everybody else, to eat, to sit down, to get the littlies ready for bed.

Her droning on about every little detail had bored her mother into submission, which taught Janet a lifelong lesson: share your own inquest on events, exhaust all avenues of probing, and save yourself from any possible inquisition.

Katherine was mumbling in her sleep in the next bed, the flat creakingly hushed, and the outside world all in bed. But Janet couldn't sleep. The struggle to join Elvis in sun-filled dreams just wouldn't lock in and stay where a story could embroider itself. Brian kept interrupting, without plot, no middle, no end.

The leaflet.

In the contortion to arrive home, ordinary and innocent, Janet had forgotten the leaflet in her pocket. Creeping down the passage to where the coats were, she fumbled in the dark for *her* coat, *her* pocket. If she woke the littlies, the whole house would be in uproar. Closing the bathroom door, she searched along the wall to find the string of the light-pull.

Shivering with cold, she sat on the side of the bath and looked at the leaflet. 15th March – Aldermaston to London CND March – Ban the bomb. On the blank side was Ben's number and address.

She heard a door down the passage open and the lugged footfall of her father coming towards the bathroom. She quickly pulled down her knickers and squatted on the lavatory, scrunching the leaflet and hiding it in one hand.

The door opened slowly and quickly shut again. 'Who's in there?'

'It's me, dad. I won't be a minute,' she whispered back.

'Hurry up, girl. I'm freezing my nuts off out here.'

She wee'd anyway; she thought she might as well, as she was there. Coming out, she reminded him that he mustn't pull the chain, kissed him, and toddled back to her room.

Shoving the leaflet under her pillow, she clambered back into the still-warm bed. 'Don't forget to take it out in the morning,' she kept saying to herself, over and over again.

'Where have you been?' Katherine whispered.

'Sshh. To the lav. I thought you were asleep. Night night.'

'No, not just now, where have you been today?'

'I can't go over it all again, you know where we went. Trafalgar Square. Now shut up, I've got to get to work in the morning.'

In the tiny silence that followed, Janet imagined herself in a duffel coat, banning the bomb. It felt good.

'Who did you go with again?' Katherine sounded very awake.

'Oh please, Kath, you know all this... Susan Lee... Now go back to sleep.'

Another silent pause, long enough for Janet to think about buying herself a black eye-pencil.

'No you didn't. You're lying.'

Lying. A quiver of electricity tingled through her. Guilt licked her soul, as she had been promised it would, ever since Sunday school. The Catholic boot camp, there to buff up her sins into a heavenly halo of goodness.

Katherine's little triumph now made way for a bigger victory. 'I know you're lying. Do you want to know how?'

Janet lay there, trying to work out what kind of person this lying business made her, but feeling all the while in a desperate state of chaos. All she wanted was a day out, for Christ's sake.

'I bet you went out with some boy, that's why you're lying, isn't it. I bet he's someone from work. Did *he* make you lie? Did he kiss you?' Katherine, getting no response from Janet, was crowing with self-satisfaction and revelling in this midnight feast.

How much did Katherine actually know? Did she spot her with Ben? Had Katherine been sent to spy on her all day? Who knew what? And how? Finally, Janet succumbed. It was more fearful not knowing the who knew what than having it all out in the open.

'If you know so much, why are going the long way about it?' Janet didn't whisper this time.

'You told everyone you were going for a day out with Susan Lee and you didn't. That's all I'm saying.' Katherine was determined to make the torture last as long as possible.

'Well, Miss Cock of the Walk, if you had something worth listening to, I'd listen. As it is, I need to get some sleep.'

They both lay there, only two feet apart in their chaste single beds, testing the air. Katherine, thirteen years old and tingling with riddles, was forced to break cover. 'Susan Lee couldn't have been with you, because... I saw her... in the Chinese... Na na ne na na.'

'You can't have. Sorry.' Janet was confident that in the closed shop, blinds down, no one would be able to see Susan and her granny scrubbing out.

'I'm telling you, you *are* lying. I was on my way round to Nan's and as I passed the Chinese...' Katherine started to chuckle. 'As I passed, there was Susan, and her nan, covered in pigeon feathers. You should have seen them. Apparently their pipes had frozen and cracked open their ceiling or something and all these dead pigeons fell out. They looked hilarious. They were both screaming the street down. I don't think their place will be open for a long while now.'

As her sister giggled away at the memory, Janet knew she would have to think up something quick. This local sideshow would be on everyone's lips by tomorrow. 'I think it is very sinful to laugh at other people's misfortune, actually. And yes, I already knew about it. Susan was supposed to come with me but of course couldn't after all that. We were both supposed to be taken round an art gallery by Eileen, this nice woman who makes the tea at my office. I did want to stay with Susan, but I would have left Eileen in the freezing cold on her own, wouldn't I?'

Janet prayed that the timing of her day-out story wouldn't be given too close a scrutiny. Then, 'What did Mum say, when you told her?'

'I haven't told her yet. Thought I'd better tell you first, so you could get your story straight. Night night.' Katherine had tested her own saintliness, that she wasn't really a wicked girl after all and could now leave any possible ramifications to the grown-ups. Within minutes she was back mumbling in her sleep.

For Janet there would be no rest that night. She went over and over the tale she had dumped on her mother of the afternoon out. Why had she mentioned Susan Lee so many times? The pigeon disaster and the Chinese shop would be talked about forever. It could even force the Lees to move away. The ingredients in the Chinese had been the subject of drunken debates since time immemorial. Cats, dogs, now pigeons.

Chapter Fifteen

1963 | FEBRUARY

Eileen, back at the ironing board, had her own visions. Did Ginger Nuts come to the flat every time she turned her back? Were Mum and Dad in on it? Have I lost him to someone like that?

This way and that, these half-glimpsed scenarios of awfulness crossed before her eyes. She could hear the old folks in the front room snoring in their armchairs, oblivious to the wireless crackling with tinny laughter, drowning out some comedy host. What was Brian thinking about in his room? Why am I standing here with nothing more to iron? Searching for something else to press?

Dear, dear Brian,
I've been meaning to mention this for quite a long time.
None of it has probably been very fair on you, but I was so worried that you would think bad things of me and cut me out altogether.

I am not your sister. Mum and Dad are not your mum and dad. They are my mum and dad.

You have always belonged to me, but I've only ever been allowed to have the shadow of you.

The lies have choked the breath out of me from the moment you arrived here.

You came out of me and I've spent the whole of your little life trying to stuff you back in.

To start again.

I can't go along with this any more, so I'll take my chances with the result of all this.

I really love you.

Eileen.

The letter had been written in a great rush. Eileen had decided this was the way the whole truth would come out, without excuses or any colouring in.

The smell of something burning and the sound of Brian running from his room brought her speeding back to the present.

'What have you been doing? Where were you? Look what you've done.' Brian had already unplugged the iron and, holding its heat away from him, was trying to splash cold water on to the ironing board with his free hand. Eileen could see she'd left the iron burning away in the middle of the board. Just forgot about it. Everything was smoking, the rose-patterned cover, the so-called fireproof cladding beneath that, all the way through to the wooden board. She picked up the teapot and threw its cold remains over the scorching. Tea leaves and brown water did a good enough job to put the smoke out, and splattered all over the kitchen table, the floor and parts of the wall for good measure.

'What the blooming heck is going on?' Rosa crimped herself into the room with drowsy eyes and sticky-up grey perm.

The crime committed and then the double crime of the tea leaves was too much for Eileen. She slumped against the door frame and, before any one knew it, was flat out on the black-and-white lino-tiled floor.

'Sis, Sis, come on, it's all right.' Brian panicked and held his sister's face, longing for it to focus on him again.

Rosa, nearly slipping over in the tea leaves, managed to get to the sink and fill a cup with tap water. 'Come on, lovey, come on, it's not the end of the world, open your trap, come on take a sip for Mummy.'

Eileen forced herself back, back to the room still shimmering with a movement of dizziness. And 'Mummy' looked so old.

'I'm really sorry… I'm really sorry about all of it.' And her eyes bled with the waters of hopelessness and isolation.

'Come on, take a sip, and Brian will get you upstairs. You need to lie down for a bit, maybe you're catching a dose of flu or something. I didn't want you to go out today in all this, did I?'

Brian's name. The letter left on her pillow. Eileen struggled to her feet and said, 'Leave me alone, for Christ's sake. I'm able to get to my room myself, thank you very much.'

Hanging on to the banisters she hauled herself as quickly as she could into the sanctuary of her freezing bedroom. The piece of paper, not yet folded, open to the world, lay on the pillow where she had left it.

Eileen took off her bootees and slipped under the heavy

eiderdown. Under the covers she folded the note in half, then into quarters, and clutched it between both hands.

Two taps on the door.

'Are you decent? Can I come in?' Brian whispered through the door. She closed her eyes and lay in silence, hoping he would go away. Stealthily, he opened the door a little, enough for him to poke his head through. She looked conked out.

Instead of creeping away, he closed the door and sat on the side of her bed. Kissing the top of her head, he put his hands under the cover and tried to find hers. Eileen opened her eyes in terror, at the same time as pulling her arms away from his.

'Whoa, calm down. It's only me,' he said.

'What do you think you're doing? Can't I have five minutes' peace?'

Brian was crushed by her roughness. He got up to leave, then decided against it. Plonking himself back down, his cold hand touched her forehead, and then gently stroked her hair.

'Give us a bit of your cover, it's like a bloody icebox in here.' He wanted her to throw half the eiderdown over his shoulders, but she didn't move, just lay there staring. He thought she was staring through him, as if he was invisible.

'Oh come on, Sis, move over, make room for one more, I need to talk to you.' He shunted her over and crawled in beside her. Barely breathing, she allowed him to rearrange her and hold her hand. With her free hand she wedged the letter under her waist. Eileen lay on her back and stared at the ceiling.

'There's this bloke who said, "I've not talked to my wife for eighteen months. I didn't want to interrupt her."'

Her sigh had a tiny laugh attached to it.

Brian always used a joke to cover up quiet moments, the

edgy moments. Gags about gammy legs before any one else could had saved him from the slaughter of schooldays.

'You do know that I didn't mean to shout at you about the iron, don't you? I was a bit all over the place, I suppose. It can't be that that's upset you, can it?'

Eileen smiled at the ceiling.

'Look, you can tell me anything. I won't say a word to Mum and Dad, I promise. Anything.'

The letter was crisp and sharp in her balled-up fist, but she ruminated on it for seconds too long.

Brian was off again. 'Is it about some bloke? Mum asked me downstairs just now if you could be pregnant or anything. Maybe you're seeing someone on the old q.t. If it is, it's alright, it's not the end of the world. I'd sort Mum and Dad out. Or is some bloke giving you the runaround. I'll sort him out, if you want me to. Just blooming talk to me.' He couldn't fathom if she was laughing or crying. Although the room was almost dark, he could see the smile on her face, see glimmers of her teeth, and what looked like puddles on her cheeks.

'I've got something I need you to have…' Before Eileen could complete her fragile decision, Rosa walked in and turned on the harsh overhead light.

'You two alright?'

They both sat up quickly from the bed.

Brian laughed and quipped how they were trying to keep warm while they had a chat.

'Oh… You feeling a bit better, lovey? Why don't you come downstairs and get warmed up?'

'I'll be down in a bit. I've got a bit of sorting out to do before the morning.' All three of them lingered in silence, not sure who was going to make the first move.

'And I found this on the stairs, is it yours?' Rosa held up the blackened silver St Christopher.

Brian was up and out of the bed in a shot. Grabbing it he said, 'No, it's sort of mine, I found it in the van the other day.'

'Well, it's not much cop, have a look at that, Eileen. Looks like it's been burnt or something.' Rosa nodded to Brian to let his sister examine it, but he pretended not to notice and, slipping it into his trouser pocket, he kissed his mum on her cheek and sidled his exit. He gave Eileen a cheeky wink and was gone, back next door to his own room. Eileen turned down the offer of a hot-water bottle and said that she would come downstairs presently.

She didn't make a move out of the bed until Rosa's footsteps had retreated. With her ear to the adjoining wall, she tried to make out what Brian was up to, but all was still and quiet in there. The letter, now scrunched up and jagged in her fist, hadn't made its rightful destination. Eileen would wait for a stronger day to deliver it.

In case of anyone rummaging about, it couldn't stay safe in the dressing table, not even in her handbag. Brian would often dig about in there looking for a nail file or scissors. Her confession was stuffed into one of her woolly gloves and put back into the pocket of her overcoat.

Chapter Sixteen

1963 | FEBRUARY

Ivy thought she would never get warm again.

The ironing board was up, making moving around awkward, and the iron was warming. Tomorrow's lemon twinset, blouse and skirt were flung over the foot of the bed, ready for pressing. The bedsit was filling with steam; gas fire turned full on, and a little pile of shillings sat on the shelf by the gas meter above the door, ready for topping up.

She clambered over the bed to reach into the chest of drawers and pulled out a flat square package of a new pair of nylons. Her thoughts didn't know which way to turn. She wanted a hot drink to warm her, she needed to shave her legs, she had to iron her work clothes, and she thought about her peculiar afternoon.

Ivy contemplated the sink in the alcove, the makeshift shaving she would have to attempt before squirming her little legs into the nylons tomorrow morning. The woman from the art gallery kept returning to her, making her feel peculiar. 'Ivy? Do you cling?' She stared out of the window at a new flurry of snow falling on to the roofs opposite.

'When will this ever end?' she asked nobody.

Poking her head out of the door, she could see that the lavatory and the bathroom were unoccupied. Ivy scurried down the hall, hoping not to come across any other tenants. It was only six thirty in the evening, but everything was still and quiet.

Of course, it was Sunday. Ivy had the entire house to herself. Everyone else had gone back to their weekend lives. She could scrape the thick ginger stubble off her legs to her heart's content, and soak for as long as the water remained hot enough.

Where did they go, those other tenants? To places that Ivy couldn't picture. Friends? Families?

The bath never took long to fill. The Ascot on the wall would supply a good six inches of scalding water spitting and farting from the taps. She closed the door to keep the steam and heat in, and then ran back to her room, quickly stripping off and donning her dressing gown, grabbing towel, soap, razor and nightdress.

Diluting this cauldron with enough cold water pushed the level to around nine inches. If she could bear to stay in there long enough, in another twenty minutes the gas contraption would be able to give her a refill. Ivy submerged as far as she could and stared at the condensation dripping off the pink and black tiles that surrounded the three walls of the bath. She thought of the people who must have passed through this house, used this bath. Except on a Sunday. She wondered how many other Ivys there were, had been, wriggling to fit in; running away from nothing, running towards nothing.

The overhead strip lighting created a corpse-like tinge on any flesh it touched. For someone as ginger as Ivy it almost bleached her away, speckling a few red patches here and there, with a greeny hue bouncing off her curly mop of hair. Pink bath, pink sink under the window; the scuffed and flaking tongue and groove panelling that reached waist-high, also pink, revealed glimpses of a deep gloss green from a previous paint job. Above the panelling, steam-proof wallpaper in a futuristic abstract pattern lined the walls. Ivy loved this design, the pink and black squares that appeared to float over the grey-green background. It reminded her of the swanky advert at the pictures for the Ideal Home Exhibition. She didn't feel quite the same about the rest of this vacant unloved room. A blushed cadaver.

Three pink shelves with curved edges, moulded in plastic, hung on the side wall near the sink, completely empty apart from a grubby, soap-dappled glass tumbler, ready for some stranger to drop their teeth or toothbrush into.

Thirty years of age. A daughter somewhere. Fifteen.

A jittery little terror swamped her pores. Looking back was depressing, and peering forward felt just as grim. Her diminished, tiny existence in Lincolnshire had replicated itself here in the city, after a decade's manufacturing of a fresh Ivy Brown. She knew that Arthur was never the dreamscape she had hatched as a future all those years ago. He was too young, had no money, probably would never have a real way of making any, and no ambition to drive towards it that Ivy was aware of. Possessing Arthur. That was what it was all about. Possessing a one-way ticket out of the flat boring Lincolnshire mud was what it had once been all about.

And now this new turn-out with Doreen.

*

Christmas was the last time she had heard anything of any interest from Lincolnshire. The good tidings had arrived inside the cheap little card with its vicious-looking robin on the front, and the yearly five-pound note.

Ivy only ever skimmed the surface of her mother's scrawl: a bounty hunter's check for any possible change in circumstances, such as a death.

Hello, Ivy love,
As I've mentioned in the card, me and your dad hope you have a lovely Christmas and want you to buy yourself a little luxury with the contents.

It's all fidgety and fuss here. Our Doreen and the lasses are going off to Australia round about February, with her new husband. We think he's a right blessing, and knocking the twins into shape, I must say.

Exciting news isn't it? Thought you would like to know.
Best of love
Mum and Dad xx

Doreen off to Australia. Ivy squelched herself into a corner of the bath so as not to get scalded, and topped up the hot water. She had almost forgotten what her only sibling looked like. Never really knew the twins. Five years since her brother-in-law's funeral. Doreen widowed at thirty years of age. That one night spent at home had been enough to last a lifetime.

She mulled on the memory of that ridiculous day. The wailing, the fainting, the whole drama of quiet people showing themselves up. Ivy hadn't ventured back since. Doreen had done very well out of Morris's accident thank you very much.

His insurance money, a widow's pension, and the cottage, completely paid for. She should be so lucky. It had felt bitterly comical going to his funeral, having never made their wedding.

Ivy rarely dwelt on her incarceration. That was another life, another being. Locked away on the farm, hardly ever seeing daylight, listening to all the comings and goings for the wedding and never hearing one query from anybody about 'Where's your Ivy?' The fifteen-year-old somewhat surplus to requirements with her fat round tummy cooking up tittle-tattle. Ivy, the suppose-to-be-bridesmaid, hidden away, out of sight. That final month, with the spooky nuns, miles away in Peterborough, waiting for the delivery, felt like a holiday camp by comparison. The nuns had dealt with the baby in spring-cleaning fashion: wiped, swiped, and was gone.

A bit like Morris. He was most definitely wiped, swiped and gone. What the combine harvester usually did with the hay, it had somehow ended up doing with Morris. He had never taken to her, and the feeling was brazenly mutual.

The only thing Ivy could think about at the funeral was, had they found every piece of him? Were all his bits in the coffin? She wasn't the only one pondering this, but she was probably the only one who found it amusing. Sweaty Alan Morris, greasy hair and pigeon-toed, as if he had just got off a horse.

Ivy lathered and razored the stubble off her legs as speedily as possible, then slid her cold shoulders back into the scummy water. She thought about Doreen's new beau, if he was local, if he resembled the departed husband.

In the pub after the burial, everyone had told her that the accident had changed old Sam Hook, whose combine it was, forever. The story was now his party piece. Three days after the event he had written to the BBC about it, saying it should feature in *The Archers*; that dramatic it being.

'Aw, no matter how I tell it, you would never believe the carnage. A corner of Hiroshima it was...' The ghoulish bought him another pint, the squeamish moved into the lounge bar and sat with the old ladies.

'You'd think it was the limbs, wouldn't you? That would be most upsetting, or the blood. But Jesus, I'm a farmer and blood is my milk and honey, ain't it? Death will defy me, as it will all of us, but that journey to heaven or hell is a B road for the likes of me.' Sam would then take a ruminating pause, his audience agog with what would fall from his chops next. He'd seen Walter Huston have a similar effect on Humphrey Bogart at the pictures and the whole performance was modelled on that.

'No, not the limbs chucked all over my field. Not even the field looking like I'd had the painters and decorators in. It was... Morris's eye... this one eye, looking up at me, eyebrow still attached, just, but now poor Morris was looking at me... and I could do nothing for the silly little bastard.'

Old Sam Hook *was* the Fens. The flat, damp squelch of drama at any given moment. Long before Morris got minced, Sam could spin a grim-reaper tale over almost anything that took his fancy, be it one of his sheep that was the spit of Mr Wilson and had this strange Yorkshire baa, or the cabbages on his neighbour's patch that couldn't possibly be right, strange cosmic glows that shone from them at midnight... Everyone was the same. That's how Ivy saw the place, and she wanted none of it. The years of listening to the deafening sound of trivia dressed up in the Almighty's clothing.

As she lay there bathing in the then, and the now, Ivy came to the conclusion that a fresh recipe needed to be invented for her life; the realization that the past ten years had been spent more or less dancing on the same spot. If she wasn't careful, she would transmogrify into her own mother, the only differences being her London address, her beaver lamb coat, the office. It crossed her mind for a split second that if her unknown daughter got herself knocked up at the same age she had, Ivy would be a grandmother at thirty. The thought shivered her to a closer grave.

Ivy had spent the fiver on a St Christopher.

Chapter Seventeen

1983 | LONDON

Eileen's special mission, the path to 10-z, her labyrinth of eternal desolation, was the longest hike of the four. The paid-for irises would be laid out there.

She delicately tiptoed over and around London's ancestry, never peered at the other non-mortals lying there in the frozen mud, wasn't interested in names, dates, beloved wife/husband of so-and-so. She viewed this whole kingdom as a vast grim housing estate of the invisibly unknown, and knew, as we all do, that this was what the living had in store.

Six irises for this one, her final errand for today: the bed of rest she had kept alive as best she could for twenty years. The three-foot-high memorial couldn't have been more different from the last one. Elegantly slim, in gleaming black marble, with a pure white, thin cross etched into it. A long slab of matching black marble lined the earth, and that was where the information on the deceased was given, also etched in white. The name in large capitals. Underneath, birth and expiry dates. Below that, at the foot of the marble, in quotes, 'Three Blind Mice'.

At the base of the headstone, on opposite corners of the slab, were two steel urns. Eileen bit off the ends of the irises, making them short enough to sit comfortably in the holes in the vases, and started to hum, as she buffed up the grave with her woolly gloves, getting rid of the grime for another week.

See how they run, see how they run…
mm, mm, mm…
Who cut off their tails with a carving knife?
Did you ever see such a thing in your life?

She always hummed the 'farmer's wife' bit, never said the actual words. On bad days she would forget what came after the first line and it would somehow mutate into 'Hickory Dickory Dock'. The journey home could be spent tortuously trying to recapture it.

'Excuse me.'

Eileen jerked with shock, banging her head against the headstone.

'Whoa, sorry, I didn't mean to make you jump. Have you hurt yourself?'

The flower-seller courteously helped her to her feet and they both stood, a little awkward with each other. They were strangers, but, after all these years, familiar.

'My sister, you know, who helps me on the stall, said it was none of my business, but it has been nagging me, and I thought I might as well mention it… Can't do any harm, can it?'

Nothing much flew into Eileen's vista at this point, but even if it had, she could never have imagined what was coming next.

'Well you've been coming here donkey's years, haven't you?

With my regular customers I do eventually discover who they've come to visit, week in, week out, and as it has never happened before, I thought you ought to know. Might be someone important to you.' He expected some response from her, or at least some acknowledgement that he should carry on. Eileen slowed her world to crawling pace, to understand what was coming next and not to miss anything.

'I can hear everything that goes on in the gatehouse, you see. Sometimes I take it in, sometimes I don't. I couldn't hear exactly what she was asking, but when I heard the gatekeeper tell her it was 10-z, the penny dropped and you immediately came to mind. I know that's one of them on your ever-expanding list. It was your very first one, if I recall.'

'A woman? What sort of a woman?'

From years long gone, Eileen had a flash of Ginger Nuts. The tiny head and overblown beaver lamb coat, with that secret skinny smile of hers. She shivered, moved a few steps, and stood on someone's forgotten beloved.

'Very smart she was. Didn't buy any flowers or anything. Called you Mrs Arthur? Are you alright?'

'I'm not married,' she said.

Eileen then did this odd thing, both her hands flat out, palms down, rubbing her headscarf on and off, backwards and forwards, making chunks of her hair poke out in all directions.

The flower-seller gently took her by the elbow and walked her out of the cemetery. With a nod to his sister to mind the stall, he steered them both towards the pub around the corner.

Eleven o'clock on a Sunday morning; the pub was just opening up.

PART TWO

Chapter Eighteen

1983 | LINCOLNSHIRE

The rain monsooned down the huge panes of glass. Ivy stared out from her desk at the front corner of the office. She had no customers yet. Beyond the window, into the high street, she could imagine the soaking flatlands of fields that lurked behind the buildings. No one will come out in this weather. An enquiry by phone maybe, but that wouldn't make her money up. That wouldn't be regarded as a sale.

Fifty years old and she was lucky to have a job at all in this climate. Moving back to London was impossible for now. This 'for now' had been hanging around for nearly twenty years.

'Ivy, your bike is still outside in all this, move it into the back passage, we don't mind.' The self-satisfied tone of her manager, all of twenty-five, blond and engaged, rattled at Ivy's cauterized heart. It was the tone of somebody attempting to be considerate to an old person. To somebody past it, like me, Ivy chafed.

She did as she was told and went out the back, knowing full well that as she disappeared Blondy would give Boy Wonder, the estate agent, and him all of twenty-one, a pursed grimace of resignation. Then he would chortle in his grubby, back-of-the-throat kind of way, rubbing his cock, gingerly checking that it was still there; Ivy being kept as ever, the rank outsider.

She had tried to make conversation with them when she first started there, about her life in London all those years ago, but they either weren't interested or didn't believe her. She had laid it on a bit thick, in retrospect a bit too thick, about where she had lived, the theatres and operas and what-not that she had experienced.

Depending on where she was with herself, Ivy's self-image would swing from smart city lady who had devotedly given up everything to care for sick and ailing parents, to a poor, dried-up old spinster, boring, plain, well past it. She knew she had never been much of a looker, but that hadn't stopped her taking some chances when she was younger. These kids here, all smuggy-boots, knowing absolutely nothing beyond this Lincolnshire wilderness, were too frightened to cross into another county unless armed with booze and a crowd for social safety.

Neither Blondy nor Boy Wonder had ever been to London, and probably never would. Ivy peered at the bike from the cover of the doorway. Even with a mad dash across the backyard she would get drenched. She listed all the plans she once had, that other lifetime ago, about learning to drive, about joining the police force. And Arthur; Arthur, who had let her have a go at the wheel of... what was the name of the firm? It wouldn't come to her, and it didn't matter now. Arthur was long gone. Driving had stopped being an obsession, stopped being the road to freedom, the moment her life changed in London.

Buff envelopes could still bring a haunted smile to her face, though.

'You alright, Ivy?' Boy Wonder had come to collect her.

'Mm? Oh yes, I'm just getting up the nerve to make a dash for it.'

'S'alright, I'll do it; only it's our lunchtime now and me and the boss are going to run to the pub. Is that okay? You can have your break when we get back. You're not going out, are you?'

Why did he have to pretend to ask? He knew, they both knew, Blondy and him, that Ivy always brought her sandwiches in. That she would sit in the store cupboard next to the lav, masticate the corned beef over and over again into swallowable gobbets. Then time to remake her face, ready for the afternoon. What they didn't know was her final mouthwash of Babycham. The secret fix to get her through the afternoon.

'Where's the bike?' Why did she always make everything sound like a crime?

'It's been raining, mother. Or have you not noticed?'

'Her Ladyship has travelled on the bus. Can't take a bit of weather,' the old girl shouted up the stairs.

Nothing. And neither woman expected it. The dad never bothered to respond to anything his wife had to say. It had always been the same, from the time Ivy was old enough to have a little look at her life out here in the Fens. Mum jawed about anything and everything, and Dad moved around in his invisible glass booth, getting on with what he felt he had to do.

He couldn't get on with anything any more. Bedridden with arthritis, incontinence, both sorts, dicky heart, and now the slow rotting of his stomach from the cancer that would probably get him first, he lay upstairs with the cat for company. Three times a day mother would visit him for the short time it took to change and feed him. Other than that, when she had a thought worth verbalizing, she would shout up, as if her brain parts needed an airing.

Ivy would see him once a day to say goodnight. She couldn't take the smell, and had never liked him anyway. Her sister, her one and only sibling, had timed her departure perfectly. Off to Australia with a brand new husband; Australia, never to be seen again. One week before Ivy's big Friday, twenty years ago.

It wasn't that big. Or it shouldn't have been. That kind of thing happens every day.

Still wearing her coat, she carried on through the kitchen out to the back door. Cowering away from the wet under the corrugated sheeting that roofed the laundry room, she lit her third cigarette of the day. One day all this will be mine, she thought. Beyond the concrete yard was an enormous field of mud. Brussels sprouts. Her father wouldn't tell anyone, least of all her, how long he had leased that field to Bert Griffiths. If mother knew, she wasn't saying. It had been at least fifteen years since her dad had worked it. She worked out that the stomach cancer would have to finish him off... in what? He surely couldn't last more than another year? And mother being nine years older than him, what must she be now? He's seventy-six... well, that makes her eighty-five. Her little glimmer of hope resurfaced. The farmhouse, the land, would be worth more than enough for another version of Ivy Brown.

Every day at work she was comparing house and land prices. She knew if she was clever about it she could make a small fortune. Timing was everything. How to sell the house on its own and the field to developers all at the same time. The new buyers would only find out too late that their backyard was going to overlook a lovely new housing estate. Ivy enjoyed the thought.

She needed to find out how long old man Griffiths had the lease on the sprout field.

'Ivy love, it's ready; yours is on the table. I'm just popping up to Dad.' Popping up to Dad might have been possible ten years ago, but now the bad hip, the enormous weight, and dodgy feet made it more of a crippled hobble than a pop. Ivy watched the great hindquarters struggle up the stairs, a plate of stew in one hand, clinging to the banister with the other.

Ivy sat at the table and faced her own plate of stew. One day, she thought, she will fall down those bloody stairs and that will be it. God willing, it will be while I'm at work and I can come home… well, not home… this is not a home… and finally get out of here. The stew was delicious, she had to give her mother that. That's all she would give her. But this was never a time to linger; eating with other people had become an indecent assault on her senses. The slurping and slobbering of the old hobbler, coughing and wheezing between chit-chatting, swallowing, and fingering any chewy bits did not conjure a picture of fine dining.

Back out in the yard, Ivy, guilt-free and vengeful, tongued her tiny teeth. She couldn't ever remember her mother having a full mouth of teeth. When she was about eleven, the class had been shown a pretty picture of the Ring of Brodgar, and that picture had always reminded her of her mother's open trap. The Ring of Brodgar, a circle of tall, ancient stones, with huge gaps between, and what looked like moss and bird shit covering their tops.

She wondered how she, Ivy, had inherited such miniature grinders. No one else in the family had seemed to. Not that they looked that small any more. A top plate of four very pearly teeth had replaced the original front rat's teeth a couple of years ago. The colour and size didn't match anything else in her mouth, but money was tight and that particular dentist hadn't shown any artistic flair. Her father's teeth had been in a glass jar for years.

'Ivy? Ivy?' The shout, getting nearer, stretched her nerves to screaming point.

'What the blooming heck are you standing out here for?'

'I worry about you, Ivy Brown, I really do. You'll catch your death, hanging about out here. You worrying, fretting about something? Come on, come in, and whatever it is, you know me, we can work it out together. I hate to see you so lonely and quiet.'

'Don't fuss, Mum, stop making dramas out of sod all.'

The ancient was crushed.

'Mum, listen to me, I've had a very important notion. You listening? Right. Well, I've been out here and having a good look at the house. It's beginning to need quite a bit of work. I mean, you've not touched it for years. It will fall down around our ears if we're not careful. So, what if at weekends we, or just me, give it a good going over? Paint job, rewiring, that kind of thing?'

'Ooh, I don't think your dad will be up for that. And where's the money coming from?'

Ivy stared just long enough for the mother to believe it was hurt that she saw. She knew eventually her mother would break the lull. 'You're being so kind and good to us, poppet, I don't want you going and getting all worried about stuff. You work hard enough as it is.'

'I want to make it more comfortable for all of us. And Dad needs a bit more, you know, his room brightening up and that.'

'Will you stop fretting? The house will be fine and it will see me and your father out. You've got better things to spend your money on, I'm sure. It's working in that estate agent's that's doing this to you. Now, come on, come into the warm, I've got a little treat for both of us. Babycham. One each. Don't say I don't think of you.'

Ivy watched her sun go down. For now. And followed her mother back into the warm.

A year. Surely no longer than a year.

Chapter Nineteen

1963 | FEBRUARY

Brian closed the front door with the tiniest whoosh and clack he could make. Six o'clock in the morning.

In Vauxhall all was quiet, with hardly anything up and about yet. Four inches of snow, and slushy bits here and there, gave the gloom a chirpy energy. In his wellington boots and brown-belted raincoat, Brian was ready to join the many: the slushers. Walking to work had become the New Year fad; it kept you warm, no freezing your bollocks off waiting for a bus that might never arrive, or down the Tube with freezing air blowing through the tunnels.

Picture-house images of sunny beaches, swimsuits and palm trees stayed where they belonged, in the back seats of the Odeon. Londoners embraced their weather at all times. Even this harsh and bitter year. After three months of freezing snow and fog, chit-chat had moved on and away from meteorological forecasting. Every relentless, boring description of the elements had been exhausted, and people were now trying to get on and live with it the best they could. Any sense of spring, summer or autumn had been buried forever under the icy pavements, as if the different seasons no longer belonged here. This had become the state of the nation.

The buses and trains were mostly full of young women office and shop workers who found the idea of walking alone in the early morning dark a risk too far; wearing what they would wear any winter, for vanity's sake, warm knee-length coat, gloves and muffler. But their exposed legs, in only thin nylon stockings, would be blue with the cold, and feet perished from the damp slush.

Workmen's outfits were more abandoned: long johns or fleecy pyjamas under trousers; shirt, jumper, heavy coat and boots, and then the wonderful display of headgear. Woolly scarf over the head, covering the ears and tied under the chin, topped off with a cap or beret. Some cheeky-chappies would then crown this arrangement with another hat, a ladies' fancy bonnet from some past wedding or other. And it did cheer people up. But a hat would destroy the careful arrangement of Brian's coiffure, and he was prepared to freeze for it.

Bandit-style, he wore his scarf wrapped round his neck, over his mouth and ears, hairdo almost untouched. The first ten-minute stride out would begin to warm him, as long as another blizzard didn't return to throw everything off kilter again, and he could look forward to the light slowly rising by the time he crossed Lambeth Bridge. The start of another week's work.

He hadn't slept that well, what with the St Christopher, and Eileen having a bit of a peculiar Sunday.

Chapter Twenty

1963 | FEBRUARY

Eileen would be the first one in.

Down the corridor from the architects' chambers, along past the stairwell, was a door that led to the post-room, a lavatory, and, eventually, Eileen's quarters. In this narrow galley, like a priest at his devotions, or some actor preparing for the limelight, she would begin her daily rituals. Coat hung up on the hook behind the door, bag, gloves and scarf placed under the red Formica table. The two-ringed gas stove would be lit and one giant aluminium kettle of water put on to boil; on the other ring an ordinary-sized kettle for more immediate tea-making. A nip to the lavatory to relift her wavy, mousy-blonde hair after the flattening by the scarf, and to push back into her French pleat any escaping hairpins. Road and Tube smuts cleaned off, eyebrows licked into shape, and a fresh touch of Gay Fuchsia brushed over her lips.

Eileen was a handsome-looking woman, tallish and square-boned with fair skin and deep blue eyes. 'Hitler would have had her breeding in no time,' the grown-ups used to comment.

Then it was back to the kitchenette. This room being on the corner end of the building gave her a large window on each wall from which to survey the streets and activities below.

From the cupboard behind the door she put on her green cotton working coat, washed her hands at the sink with the prized bar of Christmas-gift luxury soap, and checked the little alarm clock. Ten past eight. Bang on time.

Sixty cups and saucers would then be laid out and shared between the table and the trolley. By that time the kettle would have boiled and tea made, just as young Janet could be heard fumbling with the post, two rooms along.

Eileen looked forward to Monday mornings, and all her weekday mornings. The weekends for her meant interruptions and interlopers, breaking in from all corners. Parents rattling on about this, that and the other, the never-ending 'You alright, Eileen? Eileen give us a hand with this,' made having her own inner throb of private time impossible. But Monday to Friday she had her desert island, where no one entered. Unless invited.

Miss Armstrong, Val to Mr Jacobs, her boss (Valerie to her doctor), also loved Monday mornings. It was written all over her. Everybody else would arrive sluggish and beaten into their various cubbyholes of industry, as if the weekend had gulped every last drop of spirit and joy from them. The motor to get them all through another week would click in at the first chance to compare their two days off.

Up in the architects' office, the men would quietly saunter into another new week. They broke the news of their time off carefully. Over a longer pee than usual they might bring up a car-washing moment, just to filter the general mood, tentatively finding out if someone else might have had a more exciting or even dramatic time. The building bricks of every Monday morning; for the men, it was about a lot of take and very little give. The highs or lows of their tribal swaggering parade depended on which way they imagined the wind might be blowing that particular start of the week. Thankfully the subject of the weather these last few months, in all its night-mares, had aided and abetted the stories to be absolutely parallel. No one in particular being held up to derision. The usual jokes about in-laws lost in a snowdrift, not seen since Christmas, many variations on the wife not able to spend any money as she couldn't leave the house, but never much about their real selves.

Outside of this gladiatorial arena was one oddity: a good-looking bloke who lived with his mother in Walton-on- Thames, but, since the weather had really turned, was spending every weekday at a friend's flat in Maida Vale. The unnamed friend. This caused a teeny bit of jealousy: coshing him with 'Come on, Colin, you must be having quite a bit of the other... mother not around... come on, tell us your shaggy dog story.'

This Colin couldn't win either way. If he said yes, he was doing alright in that department thank you, they wouldn't leave off until they had devoured and then scorned every part of him. If he said no, nothing like that was happening, he would have to listen to their fantasies of what he should be doing with all this freedom. Mixed with 'Unless you're a poof, of course.' Much laughter, safe in the knowledge that no one in their orbit could possibly be.

Well, Colin was 'queer', and he knew when best to leave well alone.

Downstairs, the ladies in their world would also linger longer, but female manoeuvrings are quite different from the male. Tuesday to Friday, the young women would drift quickly in and out of the long narrow cloakroom, removing their hats, scarves and coats, swiping on fresh lipstick, and clacking importantly to their desks. But on Monday mornings twenty-five odd of them would hang around the sinks, warming their frozen hands in hot water or rubbing their legs to get the circulation going, and screech over each other about their two days off.

This summit conference was an open one; personal details of love, family, time spent on this, money spent on that, were for all to share and compare. Advice asked for, given, then discounted and shouted down by others, and it would start all over again with someone else's dilemma.

The posh blonde getting married to Piers would usually have a whine about the weather stopping all her fun. About not being able to get to Wiltshire for a hack on her future mother-in-law's lovely horse... then Piers already squiffy with ale by the time he arrived on Friday night... The young women who had had the pleasure of encountering Piers would give each other an eyebrow lift of 'Thank God he's not my boyfriend.' The ignorant ones imagined a pink Barbara Cartland world of heroes and wealth, and dreamt one day their prince, or Piers, would come.

Near encounters of love and romance: 'He skidded into me outside Waterloo station.' All had the fresh spark of a future that the week in the office would douse for another five days.

Ivy would butterfly-catch the ins and outs of these city girls, and every now and then chip in with something a little out of the ordinary of her own. Whenever Ivy talked about anything, it was always with a smell of secrets. She knew when to float a crumb to them and leave them with it before it could drift to the ground. It was the moment she would look at her watch, and everybody would suddenly have a vision of Miss Armstrong and warily skedaddle to their work stations. Ivy had a knack of saying much, but actually saying nothing.

Miss Armstrong had never been late in her life. She had an iron grip on herself, and her list, her recipe for living, had been tattooed into the very offal of her. Valerie Armstrong had been queen of her particular realm since birth. Her parents had run the tiny post office in the hamlet of St Godfrey's Field, not that far from Colchester. It was into this over-preening swank of the lowest branch of the civil service that she had learned the rough arts of snobbery and bullying. She absolutely knew her place in the Armstrong order of the world. Valerie could turn on a six-pence and dance the dance of a Uriah Heap for the beloved Mr Jacobs, and, without catching a breath, spin into Miss Havisham towards all those she deemed beneath her. Her ladies of the typing pool.

The Wiseman company looked after their employees in a very modern manner: the best and newest equipment, Luncheon Vouchers, two weeks' paid holiday every year, and a Christmas bonus, unheard of in British industry, was the icing on the cake. In return for these treats, the workers were kept spinning on the furious rat-wheel of the pulverizing industry.

In these months of the great freeze-up, the coldest on record since 1740, well for its duration anyway, it was business as usual for the Wiseman Pulverizer Company. Getting into work from the outside hell of snow and freezing smog made up for the tortuous journeys everyone had to make. The ancient central heating system was left on twenty-four hours a day to stop any chance of this new ice age moving into the building and sabotaging everything. Just before Christmas, two days before the holiday stand-down, Valerie Armstrong and Mr Jacobs spent the night in the warmth of the office rather than attempt the arduous trek back to Dulwich for her, and Epsom for him. The whisperings about it had come about because Miss Armstrong was seen in the same pink blouse the following day. Very crumpled. And she hadn't cleaned her teeth. Her secret cigarillo smoking had never been the secret she assumed.

The fat girl in the typing pool with the stuffed breathing and nasal honk, who had been expected by everyone to be a smog casualty, sailed through the winter with no more or less snot than previously. The posh blonde attached to Piers had worked out the answer, rather neatly Ivy thought. And bitchily: 'Well, obviously, dharling, the smog can't get anywhere near you, wouldn't stand a chance with those tubes and so-called cavities. Sometimes I do believe you are breathing through your eyeballs, the only orifices you appear to have left to you.' The confident bored tone of this, followed by a smooth turn to look in the mirror and apply peach lipstick, had silenced the entire morning mob in the cloakroom.

The rituals and customs of the outside world were pulled more into focus in the workplace. Dress codes for the particular job, regardless of the weather, were most important. No display of arm flesh, ever, even in the heat of summer; no trousers on ladies; heels of a certain height only; and hair and make-up always neatly organized. Dark suit and tie for men, laced-up shoes, no boots; bowler hats and umbrellas were optional. Even within this conventional uniform, people's lives could be imagined and to some extent worked out. Unmarried men over the age of thirty-five were either pitied or mistrusted. If he was good-looking and unmarried he was bound to be a rogue. Unmarried women over the age of twenty-five were also pitied or mistrusted. Spinsters were seen as the unforgiving face of pain.

Miss Armstrong was a spinster.

Young women moving into spinsterhood were to be avoided. They had the reputation of ensnaring men in desperate situations. They had a choice of titles: clingy, frigid, hot or passionate.

Spinsters and childless women were 'other'.

Mistresses were nearly always 'other'.

Ivy crowned herself a 'widow', but never went into the details of course.

Eileen would only mention 'widow' when pushed into it. Most of the time, no one even bothered to delve.

Chapter Twenty-One

1963 | MARCH

Janet had surprised herself as much as anyone else. She couldn't stop looking at her reflection, in the glint of the bus window, in every shop she passed.

The weather was still punishing, but there was a sense that it might soon move on to something more bearable. Every now and then she would put her hands over her ears. Her Fair Isle woolly gloves felt slightly damp. She wished she'd worn a scarf now. Italian Tony would have something to say, she thought to herself. And, of course, he did.

'G'morning, young lady, and what have you done to yourself now I ask myself? Your face will fall off in these conditions.' He craned and swivelled his neck in all directions without moving from behind the counter. He never seemed to notice that whenever his mouth formed an 'F', at the beginning, middle or end of a word, a light aerosol of spit would spray out from his protruding front teeth. He passed her the chocolate; she handed over her sixpence and retreated.

'I like my ladies with long hair, you no more my girlfriend,' he shouted after her. Janet turned at the door and gave him a twinkly happy smile.

'I sack you. You're fired,' he roared. She could still hear him chortling at his own joke by the time she was two shops away.

It had all been done on the spur. There she was looking into the hairdresser's window, trying to see their prices, and was dragged in before she knew what had hit her. And all for free, with a cup of tea and two custard creams thrown in.

Janet peeped round the arc of the corner and saw Brian leaning against the marble pillar by the entrance. The commissionaire was standing on the top step, talking down to him. Her ribs palpitated. They were expecting her, knew what time she would appear, as they always did, but she was almost on top of them before they recognized who she was.

They stared in disbelief. The awkwardness straightened up the commissionaire and he returned inside, to his post at the monumental reception desk.

'You don't like it, do you?'

From yesterday's sweet schoolgirl hairdo, kept neat and organized under her black-velvet Alice band, here she was, in exactly the same clothes, yet somehow a freshly minted wonder. Brian ogled her grown-up loveliness.

'You look a bit… French… yeah, sort of foreign,' he said. Her wide bony face, framed by this newly cropped halo of dark hair, showed off her arched eyebrows, the large warm eyes, straight nose and baby mouth.

'I know who it is, that French actress who played St Joan.'

'I never saw it,' she said.

'No, nor me, but a few years ago the advertising boards were everywhere.' He stood stock-still, looking at her as if she were some sort of Christmas-present bombshell.

'I'd better go in, else I'll be late.'

He inched closer, surreptitiously grabbed her hand to his side, kissed her exposed ear and said, 'I love it, I think you are absolutely beautiful.' Brian whistled away from her and went off to the backyard.

Eileen came across Janet in the cloakroom. 'Ooh blimey, it's you. You gave me a start there for a second.'

Janet was forensically examining her own face and new hair in the looking glass above the sinks. Eileen stood behind her and joined in the looking. 'When did all that happen?'

'Last night. I was looking in the window of Goldilocks on the corner by the college. All I did was try and find the prices, and then the man said if I came in right now I could have whatever I wanted done, but not a perm, for free.'

'What do you mean "free"? You mean nothing?' Eileen was waiting for the catch.

'I didn't know such things existed, but apparently Thursday night is model night, when the apprentices practise on real live people. They cut, they dye, they do sets and everything. Normally, you have to book, but they told me later that they dragged me in because I had such long hair and no grey in it. And my hair that was on the floor would be made into wigs and moustaches and things,' Janet said, moving her eyeline away from herself, and focusing through the mirror on to Eileen.

'I thought there'd be a catch somewhere. Real hair is worth a fortune to them. You seen the price of wigs? We had a Jewish lady here a few years back, in Accounts, right orthodox she was, and they're not allowed out in public anywhere without wearing a wig first. I was thinking getting one myself until she told me the price. What did your mum say about it all?'

Janet relived getting home last night. The nervy mumbling shock from one and all, especially from her dad, with the littlies not quite recognizing her, which had been a bit upsetting, and then Katherine asking if she could have the same thing done. That pitched the noise up a couple of decibels, with everyone shouting at the same time about 'Now look what you've started.' By the time it was bedtime an agreement had been reached that it did suit her features, but for one major complaint: it was a slippery slope now. Hairdressing was an expense none of the women in that family had ever wasted good money on before.

'I think my mum really liked it, but she was worrying about the upkeep, how much it was going to cost. She reckons I'll have to have it done every four weeks, the rate my hair grows. If I plan to leave it like this, I mean.'

Eileen pushed some clips back into her French pleat, waved her fringe out of her eyes, then washed her hands, ready for action. 'I think you look lovely. It really suits you. I'd have a go myself, but bit past it now. I'd end up looking like a prison warder.' Janet gave a moment to the idea and decided that Eileen was probably her own best judge.

'Now those architects are going to tease you more than normal today. Don't take no notice, because I know they think the world of you. Alright? Come on, let's make some tea. What do you want in your rolls today?'

Janet had a different plan for her lunch break today. 'I'm going out during the break, hope my wages arrive in time, to get some new shoes now that my haircut was free. You can't buy these sorts of shoes round my way, and I want to wear them on Sunday. Next week I'm going to look for these tight black pants that all the lady students wear.' After that mouthful, Janet felt she might have said a bit too much about herself. She didn't need the subject of Brian coming up. Eileen was always a little bit huffy whenever he was floating around.

'You married, Eileen?'

'I'll let you into my little secret. No, I'm not, but in my day, during the war, if you wasn't married by the time you were about twenty, it was the fashion to let it be thought you were a widow.' She whispered this in a saucy voice, as if she had done something criminal in the past.

Chapter Twenty-Two

1963 | MARCH

Sitting in the front seat of the van, waiting for Fred or someone to arrive who could open up the back entrance of Luderman's, Brian sucked on his skinny roll-up. What to do about Ivy? What was he scared of? She wasn't on a promise or anything.

'Come on, handsome. Time for work, put that prison finger out and let's get into the warm.' And there was Fred the foreman, banging on the van door and dragging him out. Tiny little jockey-sized Fred. He wasn't that old, not more than forty-three, but somehow had looked a little old man since he was about sixteen, would probably look like that for the rest of his days. Never a young one.

During the war, Fred had been an ambulance driver, and saw it almost as a duty to educate his young confederate on the horrors and dramas he had survived. They had a matey working relationship, but Brian always had an edgy feeling that whenever 'the War' subject was on the cards, Fred was having a little dig; a reminder of all those other young men out in Egypt or wherever, doing their National Service.

Fred wasn't having a pop at him. Fred wanted him to know that killing people is not a sport to be enjoyed, and he was best out of it all. And that Brian should thank his lucky stars for his gammy leg disqualifier.

Kettle on and biscuits out, Fred organized the cups and shouted out from the order sheets the day's deliveries. Brian did the sorting and piling on to the trolley until the kettle whistled. They would stare trance-like at the trolley-load in complete silence for the first few sips, then come back down to earth and flick through the rest of the orders, both quietly working out how many trips to the van this particular morning would require.

'Right then, bit of a roundabout today, what do you reckon? Waterloo first, then through the back to Kennington, round the Elephant, over Tower Bridge, Liverpool Street. Come back here via...'

This wasn't ever a question. Fred was organizing aloud his map and his options. Brian was following the route in his own mind's eye, privately disagreeing here and there.

By the third trolley-load out to the van, the clerks and printers were arriving, nodding their chilly noses to each other, getting the day's work up and running.

'What do you reckon vile weather smells of?' asked Fred, as he dumped himself into the passenger seat. Brian scraped the gears and moved out of the yard.

'It smells of wet wool... yeah, wet wool,' he said, looking both ways out of the alleyway.

'Wet wool?' Fred looked perplexed for a moment, then got the picture. 'Wet wool. You are absolutely right. It does blooming smell of wet wool and snot and dribble.' At the traffic lights they both put their mufflers over their noses and snorted into them like pigs. Wet wool.

The roads were just as slow, but busier than they had been for a couple of months, and Brian mooted if they would manage to complete the day's itinerary. He preferred being out and about most of the day, rather than stuck in the warehouse, but wanted to be back by the time Janet walked out the front entrance, half an hour later than Ivy. He certainly didn't want to collide with *her* for a while, not until he had plotted his final exit strategy.

'They all fancy you, those office girls, you know that, don't you?'

'Everyone fancies me, even you, Fred. Come on, own up.'

He'd contemplated broaching the Ivy affair (not referring to her by name, of course) and now Fred had opened up the subject all on his own.

'Forget about the office girls, they're a bit too lah-de-dah for the likes of me, but I do have a bit of a woman dilemma as it happens. In the mood for giving me some man-to-man stuff?' Brian took his eyes off the road for a second and shot the older man a grinning wink.

'Please don't say you've knocked someone up?' Fred said.

Brian's heart gave itself a drumming. He couldn't decide on part-truth, the whole truth, or a light opera of consequences.

'Okay, when you are fed up with one girl, even though she is very nice, and you have your eye on another one, what's for the best? That's what I'm flummoxed about. Do I let the old one down gently, by slowly seeing her less and less, or do I come straight out with it?'

'Depends on the woman,' Fred said. 'If she really loves you, then they can turn on you something vicious and cause all sorts. But if she is feeling a little bit the same, they don't seem to mind much. Are you keeping two on the go already?'

Love and Ivy had never come into it, as far as Brian was concerned. And he realized, for the first time, that maybe her longings bore no relation to his. They drove on at a snail's pace in complete silence, Brian concentrating rigidly on the road ahead.

'All I will say is, I hope all this malarkey has got nothing to do with that ginger bird in the fur coat. For your sake. She comes across as a beacon of trouble to me,' Fred said.

A bus cut across the front of their van, making a dangerous swerve in the grit and ice inevitable, and also giving Brian a chance to get his breath back from that last comment. He felt intimidated and bare in all his thoughts. As if the old man could see right through him.

'Forget it, Fred, I can't concentrate properly. Let's talk about women another time. Look at all this horrible traffic. I don't reckon we'll finish this lot today.'

At the first drop-off in Waterloo, Brian wheeled in the consignment as quickly as he could, while Fred tried to work out if a change in the route could help matters. After various consultations about this direction or the other, Fred returned to his theme. 'Being a glamour puss yourself, you probably don't notice as much I do. Must get used to girls giving you the eye. Anyway, I think you ought to know about that ginger in the fur coat.'

'I can't place which one you mean… ginger?' Brian studied the traffic, and drove off.

'Well, there you go. Exactly. I'm bloody sure it's not me she's after. She's often hanging about round the backyard. One day I asked if I could help her, she gives me the wind-up if I'm being perfectly truthful, but I couldn't help myself. Then she says, without ever looking me in the eye, "Is Arthur about?" I say to her, "Arthur? There's no Arthur here, love." See what a pal I am? It's you she's got her nails into. Arthur? I ask you. She really fancies herself, and she's got that bloody horrible whiny voice.' Fred was making man-gossip, but the casual chit-chat had reached such a point in Brian that he needed to get some of it, maybe not all of it, out in the air.

'I'm sending you a human telegram, shut your gob and let me read it out. I have been seeing her, stop. I don't want to see her any more, stop. Help, stop. How do I get out of it?' Brian suddenly quit talking and driving. Pulling on the brake, he sat back and waited.

'You forgot to put in the last "stop",' Fred said.

Brian managed a tight grin, but he was ready for more grown-up advice. He wasn't sure that Fred was the absolute oracle on romance and women, never mind, he would be better than nothing. And could be trusted. Probably.

Chapter Twenty-Three

1963 | APRIL

'You picked me up, darling, in the long run that is, therefore I'm in the exalted position.' Ivy handed over the huge bath towel and watched the long slender body step out of the bubbles.

'Be a sweetheart and percolate some coffee, and don't forget to switch it on this time, and don't fuck it up.'

If Arthur could see her now, she thought, he wouldn't believe it. It wouldn't be possible to begin to imagine it. She stared out of the huge floor-to-ceiling window, down into the perfectly groomed communal gardens. Early Sunday morning ablutions for the neighbourhood pooches were in full swing, with different coloured turds waiting to skid the unlucky. Ivy's head throbbed from last night's cocktails, exotic potions with unpronounceable names, yet all tasting of a thinner or thicker version of cough linctus.

It was a very important party, according to Pandora, but for the life of her Ivy couldn't work out important for what, or who. It wasn't a wedding or anything. It occurred in a vast house overlooking the river by Chelsea Bridge. Around forty people, of all different ages, tumbled their way up and down the four storeys, screeching at the sight of each other. Not knowing anyone other than Pandora, after a nosy poke into every room, Ivy had settled herself on a sofa by the drinks table. The drinks were being cooked up by two young black men who didn't appear to speak any English.

The only event that marked itself out was when a short, middle-aged swarthy type suddenly arrived. Everyone cheered and shouted, 'Malteser's here.' Ivy could see money being passed to him and he would give the donor a little silver nugget. It all lasted fifteen minutes at the most, and Malteser disappeared, never to be seen again.

The party had slowed down after that and most of the guests lounged, laughed, and swayed their way back into the drinks room. A dumpy little man, with short-cropped greying hair, had sidled up to Ivy and sat on the arm of the sofa and chatted her up. Oddly wearing a British Railways uniform at a posh party, he somehow didn't look as out of place as she did.

The gurgle and spit of the percolator brought Ivy back from the window. She was never sure how long to wait before turning the machine off, or when to start pouring it out.

'Okay, sweetie, that's the signal, turn the fucking thing off.' And there stood the spick and span Pandora, dressed only in a pair of lace knickers, carrying an armful of clothes.

'Don't get too close to the window, people will see you,' said Ivy.

'I want them to see me. I'm their Sunday morning church bells. Didn't you know?'

Pandora dumped the clothes on to an armchair, framed her

whole self in the window frame, first backside on and then front. Yawned, stepped away, and sashayed towards the coffee. She looked for all the world like someone holidaying on a hot beach and needing to stretch their legs.

Ivy studied the other woman's rear view as if she were measuring her for a coffin. Every detail of Pandora's perfect length, shape, skin, absorbed.

'Was his name really Celia?'

'Oh, you are such a clodhopper, Ivy. Honestly, you are the end. Celia is not a *he*, Celia's a girl!'

'But she looked like a man last night... well, to me anyhow. And why did she dress up as a railway guard?'

Pandora had got herself a coffee, completely ignoring one for Ivy, and sprawled herself over the clothes on the armchair.

'Ceals has always been like that. She loves uniforms. She was the only girl at our school delirious about wearing the stupid hat. Even the knickers, and they were hideous, let me tell you.'

'She's not like any of your other friends,' Ivy said.

'You haven't met my other friends.'

'What about all those people at the party?'

'Well, we know them, but they're not friends, more like rellies actually; you know, second cousin to last stepmother kind of thing, or from school.'

Ivy finally moved from her spot and got herself a cup of coffee. She had experienced a whole new situation these last few weeks and was struggling. She kept her back to the room.

'Does this Celia think she's... or wants to be... an actual man?' She could hear Pandora pulling on clothing and slowly getting together for the rest of her day that may or may not include Ivy. Ivy would wait to be asked.

'No, no, of course not. Who'd want to be a man when you don't have to be? We all had a crush at some time or other for Miss Faraday, our RI teacher. It would last at most a couple of terms and then you moved on to someone else. We just presumed that Ceals was still in love with her. It didn't matter a jot, of course. But it wasn't that at all. I found out one ghastly orienteering day, when we decided to get purposefully lost and holed ourselves up in the warmth of some tea lounge in this cheap and nasty hotel... What time is it?'

'Quarter to twelve. What are you looking for?' Ivy saw Pandora, now fully dressed in tight black ski pants, black roll-neck sweater, digging around the padding of the armchair.

'Christ, I've got a headache. My pearls, I've dropped them down here somewhere.' Giving up the search for the moment, she planted herself back on the chair and waited for Ivy to refill her outstretched coffee cup.

'If it wasn't the RI teacher, who was it? You?' Ivy returned and sat on the floor.

'Ethel Smythe. Can you believe it? Poor little Ceals obsessed with Ethel Smythe?'

'Was she another teacher?'

'I called her Ethel for a while, she loved it. But people found out and stopped us. I should go back to it really... poor old Ceals. It's like being obsessed with Elvis or something. No, Ethel Smythe was this hideous Edwardian composer, very rich, bit of a hanger-on with the suffragettes and all that. God knows how a twelve-year-old got the illicits for her. The music is vile. And not a pretty woman by anyone's standards. Anyway, when Ceals is conducting her human traffic down at Waterloo station, in that lovely serge uniform, she feels musical, sexual, historical and important, and that's all that matters to me.'

'Have you got anything to eat?' said Ivy.

'Here? No. I'm going to meet up with Ceals at the Dorset Arms for hair of the dog and some eggs, I think. You can tag along if you want.'

Ivy's hangover finally reached her stomach and she made a dash for the bathroom. When it was all over she sat on the side of the bath and scrutinized herself in the cruel full-length mirror opposite. Cruel, because the only other image in the room was a full-length photograph of Pandora stuck on to the back of the door. Sitting on a zebra-skin throne, completely naked, fingering a ukulele.

Ivy didn't have the imagination to compare body lines. For her, elegance was all to do with clothes. She stared at her now crumpled grey skirt and pink blouse buttoned to the neck, her blue pointy-toed shoes with the little heel. She felt she had turned, overnight, into Miss Armstrong, all safe and dowdy, old before her time. She needed to get home to the secrecy of the bedsit, have a bath, clean her teeth, and prepare for tomorrow. If she saw Arthur in the morning maybe she could flounce about her weekend with rich people. That would put him in his place; that would make her more elegant, more desirable.

'Better?' Pandora, blotting her violent red lipstick on an old envelope, didn't look up from the compact mirror.

'I think so… erm… I need to get back home now. Clean my teeth and stuff. Have to get myself organized for work tomorrow. Thank you for a nice time.'

Perusing Ivy, Pandora said, 'You have the tiniest teeth in the world. Just like a piranha's.'

*

Ivy didn't have a bath. Instead, she locked herself in her room, put the fire on, made spaghetti on toast and a cup of cocoa. Where was Arthur? She thought about everything she had done to please him, keep him. Every day for the past, what, four or five weeks? Ivy had mulled over what had changed, and it always came back to the same scenario. The little post-room girl. Arthur having someone else was too savage; everything dangerous, unpredictable, and perilous, for all three of them.

And now the beginning of this new set-up with Pandora.

Two weeks after their first encounter, Ivy returned to the Tate, saw Pandora, and shyly reintroduced herself. All that had happened beyond that was going for a drink around the corner a couple of times, and the exchange of bits of information about themselves. Not too much information from Ivy. Until Saturday night. The party invite.

She could remember everything about the party, the last whoops of goodbyes; she could remember the luxury of the black cab outside afterwards, and the address. World's End; somewhere she had never been in all her ten years in London. Then nothing. Until this morning. As far as Ivy was concerned, particularly in this case, if she couldn't remember, then nothing happened.

She pondered on what Pandora and Ceals would make of the post-girl. If that should be her next move; take the post-girl out of Arthur's heart and hand her over to another life.

The first sleep came quickly, but only lasted a few hours. Backwards and forwards to the lavatory, her following shallow sleep brought dreams of resolution, answers to all things incomplete. Arthur's face swirled into the post-girl's and folded up as one. Black glossy hair and shining eyes evolved into eleven-year-old Ivy's cat, Gossip. Gossip, who she had fussed and loved and had her private moments with, one day had moved into Doreen's room, and from then on became Doreen's companion.

It had taken a lot of planning, and that was what Ivy was always most proud of: the perfection of it, the secret of it.

The day after her thirteenth birthday, a Wednesday afternoon, sitting on the forbidden shale bank half a mile from the station, with Gossip in a fierce, hateful grip under her school uniform, the 4.20 from Grantham came racing through the town. The train didn't even make a judder on impact. As if Gossip had never existed.

Chapter Twenty-Four

1963 | APRIL

April had at last arrived and spring was beginning to show off a bit. The harsh winter had sent everybody a little doolally. Earning money in the construction business had been nigh-on impossible. Repairing crashed ceilings from frozen pipes, caved-in and fallen-over walls, kept the wolf from the door, if you were lucky. William Brady had been more fortunate and busier than most.

It was time for a serious sit-down. William felt in his bones that his house and its inmates were no longer on intimate terms with him, and hadn't been for some time. The whisperings, slammed doors, not everyone accounted for at the supper table, and the whole household negotiating with him at arm's length for reasons best known to themselves: he needed to get to the bottom of it.

'Where's Katherine?'

Maureen concentrated on the rinsing of the plates. Her back was to him, but she recognized something was up and that he wasn't going to shift until he got his answers.

'In her room, where she always is these days. Why? What do you need?' she said.

'I want her out here. Now. And what about Janet? Where is she?'

'You know where she is. She goes up to that art gallery of a Sunday. You should take a bit more interest, then you'd get no surprises.'

Maureen was chippily getting ready for something. She wasn't sure which way any of this was going to go, whether to play the innocent, be defensive, or shut him up with a row and then some tears.

William marched out of the kitchen and, without warning, flung open the bedroom door.

'In the kitchen, young lady,' was all he said, as he stomped back to where he'd come from.

He unravelled bits from time to time, and whenever it looked like he might be getting somewhere they would babble him back into confusion. All this was performed with an instinctive sense of protection. But Maureen and Katherine had no idea themselves what they were protecting. The Chinese friend round the corner got a mention, overtime and possible promotion were thrown into the ring, along with Janet's passion for the art gallery. But William was having none of it, and just to prove a point in his own mind, he said he was going to the Chinese shop to question Susan Lee himself, and ordered Katherine to accompany him. And that was that.

Back at home, all of them realized that whatever cat had been in the bag would very soon be out; exposed to the full glare of the family.

Katherine lay in the dark trying to hold her breath. She heard the 'night night' from the other room, her mum and dad not even mentioning the afternoon's drama, as if all was as is. She heard her big sister come in, creep out of her clothes, into her nightdress, and slip under the covers. She waited long enough for Janet to feel relaxed.

'You're really in the shit now,' she whispered.

The tingle of joy Janet had felt all that day wired itself into a fear. Little sister was not going to let her rest.

'What? What have you been telling them?' She leapt the few inches' gap between the beds and pinned Katherine's shoulders to the pillow.

'Get off me, get off, I'm trying to help you. I haven't said anything.' Katherine struggled for breath and shoved herself free.

The next two hours were spent cuddled together, going over and over what might be their parents' punishment, and what would the punishment be for. Having your own secrets? Lying? Pretending to go everywhere with little Susan Lee?

'Will you keep on seeing him, even if Mum and Dad say you can't?'

'I have to... I love him, I think.' Janet remembered the tingling pin-pricks of heat all over her whenever his hand touched her shoulder, his skin grazed hers, or the side kiss he would lightly brush on her. His lips catching her, half-mouth, part-cheek.

She fell asleep in Katherine's embrace, dreaming of Brian's violet eyes and beautiful face. Having forgotten those film-starry nights only months ago when Elvis would come to comfort her. Elvis had phantomed into air, gone forever.

Chapter Twenty-Five

1963 | APRIL

Janet left the house that Monday feeling as old as Grandma Lee. The lightness, the quickness, of her step belied the heavy rocks rolling around her guts. No interrogation from anyone so far, but she knew it must be brewing.

It was such a lovely seven o'clock, with the sun perforating through the morning's ether, that she decided to walk off her nerves and have a long think. After about half an hour, working her possible problems this way and that, she had reached St Paul's Cathedral. Another ten minutes and she would be there.

'Ay, my gorgeous, Tony no good enough for you any more? You walk right past me today? I do something wrong for you?' He had made her jump. There he was, standing in his doorway with the bar of chocolate. Janet rummaged her coat pocket for the sixpence.

'Pay me tomorrow… you going nowhere are you? You little bit later today.' He gave her a saucy wink and went back into his shop.

She was late, not enough late to get into bother, because if any one was in before her, it would only ever be Eileen. Eileen might proffer some Mum and Dad advice as well as a cup of tea this morning. Then, maybe not. Eileen had always been a bit rattled and surly about Brian's appearances up Wiseman's back stairs.

And there he was, leaning against the front entrance, smiling that smile of his and tapping his wristwatch. 'I've been here half an hour, I should be putting the world to rights with my envelopes and compliment slips, and what do you do? Stroll in without a care in the world. I don't know, kids of today.'

Janet was frozen to the spot, in awe. Daylight seemed to bounce off him and blind her senses.

'You alright?' he said, and came towards her, so close. Too close. Her eyes poured water. Brian looked about him, for safety's sake, then folded his arms round her, vanishing her into his little short jacket.

'Oh blimey, what's the matter? I didn't mean anything.'

'I'm frightened. Really frightened,' she said.

He spread his brains for a clue as to what she was talking about. She moved out of him, and, looking down the street, avoiding any eye contact, said, 'I'm frightened of everything this morning. And I'm really frightened of you.'

That hung in the air for the pair of them.

'You can't be frightened of me. You mustn't. You can't.'

'Oi!'

From out of the sky, three floors up, a window had scraped open and there was Eileen, peering down at them. 'You're a bit late this morning, Janet, you better get your skates on… And you, mister, should be round the tradesman's entrance, not messing about round here.' The window was slammed back down and she was gone.

Brian laughed. 'Don't worry; it's only my sister being old bossy boots,' he said.

'Sister? She never said a word. Ever. I thought she liked me.'

'This is not about you really. This is about… well… don't take this the wrong way or anything…' It was the first time Janet had ever seen him lost for words.

'I can't believe she's your sister and neither of you mentioned it. What else haven't you mentioned? You've both been laughing at me.' Her whisper was full of imagined humiliation.

Brian grabbed her wrists to stop her trembling. 'Calm down, get to work as normal. I'll wait for you when you've finished and have a proper talk.' He skipped away to the corner before Janet had a chance to tell him that she mustn't be late home, not tonight.

'I LOVE YOU, JANET BRADY,' he shouted down the street.

Chapter Twenty-Six

1963 | APRIL

William Brady, at over six feet tall, with large head, feet and hands growing out of him, was not an easy specimen to hide. His cruise around Holborn to get his bearings had been going on for about half an hour and he trusted, because she had no reason to expect him to be there, she wouldn't spot him. William had tortured himself over Janet's possible offences, but was beginning to feel slightly crude about actually spying on her. He found a bus stop, on the other side of the road to Wiseman's grand entrance, slightly at an angle, to loiter and watch.

He noticed a skinny, dark-haired young man leaning against one of the marble pillars to the left of the front door, obviously waiting for someone. After about ten minutes, a short ginger woman came dashing out. She looked overwhelmed by the heavy brown fur coat she was swaddled in. William watched as the young man appeared to try and get the woman to move away from the entrance with him, at the same time looking beyond her for something, or someone. More people started to filter out, but no sign of Janet. Two buses sliced right across his view, and he was almost pushed into the road as the queue behind barged him out of the way. By the time the buses had moved off, a tiny drama was unfolding opposite.

The fur-coated woman was clinging on to the lapels of the young man, as he tried to pull her off him. The commissionaire came out and got involved in the upset, which didn't seem to have any effect, when a few seconds later Janet appeared. She stood there staring with absolute shock at what was in front of her. The young man shouted something that William couldn't quite catch, gave her three nods that looked like directions, and Janet ran off down the street. Whatever was going on here was far more serious, William decided, than all his previous concoctions, and this could only be unravelled by stalking the boy.

Janet's version could wait, for now.

Chapter Twenty-Seven

T he U-shaped garden was surrounded by a circus of rush-hour noise. The only other inhabitants of the churchyard were the long dead, and two squiffy tramps, having a highfalutin pontification about South Africa, completely unaware of any-one else in the early evening gloom.

'Well, one thing's for sure… we don't contribute a brass farthing to their economy… can't be blamed for a thing there. I can't contribute a brass farthing to my own economy, can I? What's to boycott? I do love that word.' The ragtag of a man stretched to the cider bottle and took a deep, erotic swig, and passed it over to his female companion.

'Cricket? You are very happy with their cricket,' she accused him, before taking her own glug of the nectar.

Brian was out of breath, and before anything else, before he had a chance to sit down, Janet asked him what the time was.

'Quarter to six.'

'I'm really late now. Something's up at home.' She stood, ready to run.

'I've told her, it's over. It's been over since Christmas really, but she won't leave me alone. I love you. YOU. Me and Ivy were about something else. I'm not sure what, but that's that.' He sounded aggravated.

'So frightened,' she said.

'This is hallowed ground, do you mind, we won't have any bestial pleasures or violations here, young man,' the lady tramp shouted over. Her fellow traveller cackled, took another swig and laid back on the granite table of the deceased. Janet nervously peered at them, hoping not to catch their eye and any further commotion. In the gloom, she was aware of shadow movement over by the trees near the wall. Something or someone was creeping around. She thought it might be a policeman, watching the drunks, and it crossed her mind that maybe nobody should be in the churchyard at this time, maybe they would get into trouble as well. He watched her staring into the distance, silent. Her nose started to run, and he saw she was crying.

'If this is about that bloke I met yesterday, your foreign blokey, then tell me now. You promised me you were just mates, but if it's him you want... yeah, I am jealous and all that... and if he's laid a finger on you, I'll knock his fucking lights out... Sorry, sorry, I didn't mean that... please say some-thing to me...Why do you always look away when I'm speaking to you? Are you messing about with me?'

She slowly turned her head and braved herself to face him. As if there was some horror waiting there, some lightning rod from God ready to blow out the lights.

Chapter Twenty-Eight

1963 | APRIL

Ivy remembered reading somewhere the recipe for a perfect life: Love, Money, Work. The three necessaries for a state of bliss. Two of them, in any combination, could equal happiness. Having only one of them would equal not much, discontentment. None? Not worth thinking about.

She sat watching the pushing and crammings of Londoners desperate to get into the carriages and home before tea. The Tube whooshing off into the darkness. That nosy parker commissionaire. Who else had witnessed the uproar? The thought of work tomorrow pumped her hot and cold. That post-room girl.

She was on the platform going east. Her bedsit was north; Pandora, west; and Arthur was anonymously south. The entire compass of her existence.

Ivy erased Arthur's final words and her brain retyped them in a different order, the way it should have been. She heard the crackling power of electricity hop and somersault through the tracks, as a train coming from the opposite direction was about to thunder into the station. She thought of the 4.20 from Grantham. The sitting and waiting on the shale with Gossip. The standing up, the stretch of the throw, the perfect timing. It had been exhilarating; so exciting. She'd stayed on the shaley slope for half an hour, hoping that some stray might be around and she could do it all over again when the 5.10 screamed through. Doreen's little misery, the tears, refusing to eat until Gossip returned, gave Ivy two of the most pleasant weeks of her childhood. She would leave cartoons of a steaming, cauterized cat, flattened out on the railway line, on Doreen's bed.

Two weeks of misery, then all is fine with the world. That's how it works. It was that post-room girl after all.

The sound of another Tube train, and then the crunching, grinding and scraping of heavy steel coming to a standstill as it stopped, for its own mysterious reasons, in the tunnel. She changed platforms and travelled west.

Pandora was out. Or too idle to answer the door.

Chapter Twenty-Nine

1963 | APRIL

Eileen laid out birth certificates, death certificates and marriage lines. Small square black-and-white photos from the family Brownie camera were put to one side of the bed. This box of family heirlooms, kept for whose safe keeping? thought Eileen. One lie could cover or aggravate so many others.

'Eileen. It's half past seven, love. Is Brian going to want this when he gets in or shall I turn it off?'

'I don't know, Mum, I'll be down in a minute... Leave it for a while.'

The photographs, unlooked at, were thrown in first, on top of two ration books, Granny Joyner's gold earrings, and a long-gone relative's lace christening cap. The records of existence, neatly folded, placed on top. Eileen locked the box and returned it to the bottom of the wardrobe. The key was dropped in the little yellow dish on the chest of drawers.

That morning's shout out of the window to him had jangled her all day. He'd never attempted to come and find her, for which she was grateful; it had been hard enough keeping face with Janet at tea break. Neither of them had touched the subject; it wasn't mentioned. But Brian wouldn't be able to let it be when he got home, she was sure of that. And what *had* it all been about? Eileen didn't entirely know herself, only that she couldn't lose him to someone else just yet.

'Eileen, I think this water's boiled dry. Shall I put some more in?' Rosa's voice could cut Vauxhall with a knife when she had a mind to.

'Mum, I'm coming. Stop shouting.'

Rosa lifted the warmed-up dinner off the top of the steaming saucepan with a double-folded tea towel, but that was still not thick enough to prevent a scalding. Eileen arrived at the kitchen door to see Brian's dried-out lamb chops, potatoes and peas all over the floor, speared with triangles and shards of exploded plate.

'Oh bloody hell... bloody hell,' Rosa was hopping about on one foot and trying to shake her hand into a coolness.

'Oh Mum, for Christ's sake, why couldn't you wait for me?' She dragged Rosa's hand under the cold tap and focused on the plughole.

'Where's Dad?'

'Down the pub. Darts, thank Christ.' Rosa hobbled from the tap and sat with a wet dishcloth wrapped around the traumatized hand.

'Oh, lovely. Dinner on the deck now, is it? Shouting and hollering this morning, showing me up in front of the city and gawd knows what, and now this, what the bloody hell is going on here?' Brian made them both jump.

'Don't start... it's all my fault. Our Eileen's not stopped since she's been home from work, and now look what I've gone and done. Scalded myself and everything,' Rosa said.

Eileen was on her hands and knees, cleaning up the mess with a pan and brush. She didn't look round, didn't acknowledge him.

'Come on, you two, not the end of the world. Got any Spam? I'll have a Spam sandwich or something, I'm not really that hungry, tell the truth.' Brian shoved Eileen out of the way, and cleared the ashes of his dinner himself.

'You been drinking?' Rosa said.

'Yes, I have, as a matter of fact. Been a most unusual day. First I was up, then down… then down a bit further… and now I'm right up again. I decided to celebrate with myself.'

Rosa laughed. He gave Eileen a wink, which made her melt and smile. She winked back at him as he put the remains in the bin under the sink.

'Actually, you two, fancy a little drinky poo on me? Come on, I want another bevvy. My treat.'

'Not for me, boy, you and Eileen go. They'll have a sausage roll or pastie or something for you as well there, soak the booze up,' Rosa said.

Apart from four old girls, the lounge bar was empty. The old women sat wrapped in their coats and hats, clutching their handbags firmly to their laps, sitting side by side on the old chintz banquette near the lavatory. When Brian and Eileen came in they all gave a tiny nod of recognition, and turned their previous volume down to a private level. The long, narrow bar was lit by four white glass globes, high in the ceiling. The harshness continually echoed as the light bounced off the mirrored walls. Along one side, opposite the counter, were various arrangements of little round tables and chairs. Up in the far corner, furthest from the old ladies, were a couple of battered armchairs. Eileen chose the last table, while Brian went and ordered.

They could hear the darts game going on in the snug the other side of the lavatories, and every now and then cursing, followed by laughter. Most of the noise coming from their dad. She watched Brian treat the old girls to a bottle of beer each; watched as they made a fuss of him, told him he was a handsome bugger, and asked if he was spoken for. He came back to her twinkling, doing exaggerated strides on tiptoes, trying to avoid landing too many times on the pub's gluey carpet, his diminished right leg interrupting any chance of a rhythm.

Brian clinked his half-pint of Mackeson's against her glass of Babycham, then sucked up an enormous glug so loudly he made himself laugh and choke on the reflux. Bubbles of beer blew out of his nose. A piss-take on the way their dad always attacked his mug of tea, with a big inhaling slurp. Eileen joined in, violently siphoning a thin whistle of Babycham into her mouth. The shock of fizz and alcohol, which she wasn't used to, brought on a spumy coughing fit, and Brian had to bang her on the back a few times.

'Oh Christ, thought my eyeballs had fallen out.'

'Have you never had a bloke? A boyfriend or anything?' Brian asked her right out of the blue.

'Wouldn't you like to know.' She tapped the side of her nose, giving off, but not giving up, any supposed secrets. He waited for more. Nothing came.

'I bet you hear all the office gossip on your tea rounds, don't you,' Brian said.

'I don't see how. Nobody says a word. I'm invisible up there.

I don't miss much, though, if I keep my wits about me. And if it's of any interest, of course. To me, that is.' Eileen had a feeling where the conversation was going, and wondered if it would have gone down the same path if Mum had been with them.

'Well, you'd better be prepared for some gossip tomorrow,' he said.

Eileen took a tiny sip of her drink and trapped herself in the mirror opposite. I've never been on intimate terms with myself, she thought, but now this face is a complete bloody stranger to me.

'What are you thinking about? You staring at yourself.'

She pushed an imaginary hairpin back into her untidy French pleat. 'I'm thinking of getting my hair cut... maybe dyed... bring back my blonde locks. Won't notice the grey as much then.'

Brian scrutinized her and said, 'You're not grey, you must be looking at somebody else.'

They both shot a look at the old girls at the other end and grinned. Both ancients in the middle of the group had conked out, and the ones at each end were whispering over their rumpled bodies. 'My future, if I don't watch out,' Eileen indicated the pensioners.

'Give us a cuddle.'

'What's it worth?' she asked.

'I'll tell you my secrets, if you tell me yours.' Brian put his arms around her anyway, and kissed her ear.

She couldn't quite get a handle on his mood. He was ready to play about and have fun, but a lot more was going on with him. 'This could be really embarrassing, and I'm hoping that my foreman can help me out if the shit does hit the fan.'

'Best spit it out, then.' Eileen didn't take her eyes off his untouched meat pie, now cold.

'I don't know where to start, if I'm honest.'

She looked at him through the mirror opposite, but from that angle at the table his face hit the bevel in the glass, splitting and fragmenting his features.

'I feel like I've been through the hoop today, you hanging out the window like old Mother Riley this morning… No, shut up, let me carry on. Right. I was waiting quite innocently for Janet, you know Janet, your post-room girl, when before I knew what hit me Ivy comes out and starts shouting and hollering the odds. That brought that miserable old bastard commissionaire to the door. People in the street are looking at us and everything; Ivy's hanging on to my coat. It was a nightmare. Then Janet appears, she gets an earful, and I try and get her out of there fast. Most of the office staff were witnesses to all this as well, and your guv'nor, I think, sorry to tell you.'

Brian said all this in a fast, low key, checking around him at the old girls at the end, and to see if the barman was about and earwigging. Eileen stared at the pie.

'Well, say something,' he said.

'Who's Ivy?'

'Oh come on, Sis, you know full well who she is. You drop enough hints about her. That ginger fucking midget in the office.'

Eileen was back gazing at herself in the mirror. Brian took her hand for comfort, but she snatched it away. There was nothing more he could think of doing, he stood up and went off to the lavatory.

The noise from the darts match next door filtered through.

She could hear her dad shout something about 'You can't count, you silly old fucker, you've not written it all down… you've missed out my fifteen.' For some reason this flew her back years to the hospital; that terrible time, twelve years ago, when she thought she had lost Brian, again. Waiting for hours in that green and cream side room, the overhead strip lighting smacking you in the eyeballs with the hard lines of reality. Watching withered men down the corridor in their blue tartan dressing gowns, playing darts, the last game left to them before they died. Waiting for permission to have a glimpse of Brian's mildewed scrag of a body. All that medieval-looking technology trying to keep him alive, unable to comfort, speak, or touch him.

She heard his footfall return. Whenever he was over-tired or anxious, the right leg was less well behaved. The polio releasing him, but leaving its autograph for ever. Poliomyelitis.

'She pregnant? This Ivy?' Eileen had said it before he'd had a chance to sit down.

'What?…. Oh Christ, no. Don't say that. Christ Almighty.'

The way he fell into his seat, the way he let his head fall on to the table, defeated, told her all she needed to know. She would lose him before she ever owned him, and felt sick.

Chapter Thirty

1963 | APRIL

J anet's lips were near-paralysed from the brunt of his kiss. She ran her tongue this way and that behind her front teeth to stop the jarring, and her face from aching. She was over an hour late, bedevilling the situation by deciding to walk home. Was it to be more fibs and contortions, or straight out with all of it? Panic warping into resentment.

This winter had altered so many things. Elvis, flown away to some other schoolgirl's dreamland, who had touched her body during sleep, where only she had touched herself before. Dreaming now of Brian touching those places, mortifying her at the same time with a Holy Mary shame. And Ben. Kind, brave, clever Ben. Teaching her marching songs, talking about America, bombs, Amsterdam, and real coffee. How big the world should be. Could be.

Janet slammed the street door behind her, determined to let them all know she had arrived, not creeping in like a school kid. It was eight o'clock. The bang shook the littlies awake in their cots. Katherine came out of her room and peered down the stairs, screwed up her face in alarm as a dire warning, and then, at the sight of Maureen poking her head round the kitchen door, hurried across the landing to settle the babies back to sleep.

They were suddenly face to face by the kitchen door.

'What time do you call this?' Maureen scrutinized her daughter for any signs of damage.

Janet's secondary school, with its fine-tuned brutality, had managed to educate the local Catholics with a certain flair for battle. When necessary. 'I reckon it's about seven o'clock, don't you?' Janet flushed at the sound of her own tone, and wasn't sure how far she could play this, but was ready for a bruising. They stood quietly eyeing each other up for a few seconds. Maureen gave a little knowing nod and went off into the living room. Janet valiantly followed, and twiddled with the three-quarters-finished jigsaw laid out on the sideboard.

It was a scene of the money-changers in the temple, one of Katherine's Christmas presents. Dazzling, crude, overdone blues and reds, turbans, robes, donkeys, stalls upturned, and there in the centre the glowing Jesus, with daggers of heavenly light piercing out of him. In the upturned lid of the jigsaw were about a hundred and fifty pieces, bits and bobs of sky, stone pillars, merchants' faces.

> Don't you hear the H-bombs thunder
> Echo like the crack of doom
> Whilst they rend the sky asunder
> Fallout makes the earth a tomb.

Janet mumbled the dirge, above a hum, but not too loud for over-attentive ears. Twenty, thirty minutes of this near-silence.

They both, for different reasons, hoped that Katherine would stay where she was, out of the way.

It was nearly eight thirty and Maureen was popping with agitation. But she had been given strict orders to keep her mouth well and truly shut until William was ready to deal with it all. She moved the clothes horse from in front of the hearth and concentrated on folding the dried washing; doing it as slowly as possible, filling time, waiting for the key in the door. She debated whether to chance leaving the room and put the clothes away in their rightful places, or stay put and just wait.

'Where's Dad?'

'He'll be in soon, now that you're back.'

Movement from upstairs. Sounds of Katherine leaving the littlies and making her way downstairs, then a change of heart as the front door opened and slammed. She stayed out of it and went to her room. Two coughs and he was there.

William surveyed the living room, saying nothing. Just stood in the door frame in his huge black overcoat, blue beret with the leather trim covering most of his short curly grey and black hair. He bent down where he was and took off his concrete-powdered army boots, usually a job that the kids fought over on any normal day. The first words he said were to Janet.

'Why have you still got your coat on? Going out somewhere?'

'I've not warmed up yet,' Janet said, not looking at him, and carried on searching for another piece of jigsaw.

'I bet you haven't.'

William took off his overcoat and handed it to Maureen to deal with, along with the boots. She wasn't happy about this silent order to leave the room. 'We've all had ours, but yours and Janet's is a bit dried up now. Would you like egg on toast or something?'

'No, thank you. When I'm ready Katherine can get us both a Chinky from Janet's best friend, can't she? Oh fuck, they're not open on a Monday are they?'

Maureen left them to it.

Janet sidled to the end of the sideboard, still studying the jigsaw, but now with her back to him. He padded over to the fire, gently manoeuvring the pile of newly folded clothes, and sat on the square brass coal box by the fender. William had bothered himself this way and that, all the way home, whether he was making a mountain out of a molehill. Sitting here with her, he wasn't that sure of himself, if he should come on all heavy-handed over what might be kid's stuff, growing up stuff.

'What's all this art gallery lark? This going there every Sunday, apparently. Is it where you go?'

Janet stopped, slowly took her coat off and hung it over the back of a dining chair, and sat completely upright at the table. As stiff as a board, she faced him full on. 'I say I go there every Sunday, therefore I do. Where else should I go? Why would I lie about it?'

'Well, my little darling, because people do lie from time to time. And, as you well know, me and your mother cannot abide liars.' If she hadn't been in such a spin she would have laughed at his schoolmistressy tone. Janet had never heard him sound so big and so little in the same breath.

'Do you have a favourite picture? Or do you mooch around looking at all of it? I could do with a bit of sophistication myself, maybe I'll join you next Sunday. Would you like that?'

Janet found this was the perfect chance to diffuse whatever

bomb he thought he was holding over her. 'You can come if you want, but I never said I go *inside*. I hang about on the wall by the fountains and chat to all the students. Mum must have told you that I'm always asking Katherine to come with me, but she's not interested.'

That flummoxed him, he'd never expected that, and she knew he hadn't. William pondered on the good-looking boy, the ginger fur-coated woman, and his daughter, all having some sort of debacle in the street, showing themselves up for all to see. Whatever it was all about, it must have been important and, more to the point, important with dangerous features. The boy didn't have the way of a student, not ones he'd seen in the newspaper anyway.

'Dad, do you mind telling me what all this is about? Everyone round here's been a bit funny with me for weeks now.' There, she'd said it, and it hadn't scared the wits out of her.

The jigsaw had not been a wasted diversion. It had allowed her the time to jig all the possibilities of her supposed sins. And whatever was going to happen, after tonight and Brian and the graveyard, nothing and nobody was going to stop her from being with him, for as long as she could keep him. She put her index fingers to her lips, conjuring up his softness and his smell.

Maureen couldn't stand it a minute longer, she'd occupied herself in the kitchen long enough. 'I'm sorry, William. Come on, let's get straight to it. Why are you lying to us? Number one. Why say you go out with Susan Lee when you don't? Number two. Why are you always late home from work these days? Number three. Let's start there, young lady, shall we?'

Janet laughed, then blushed into giggles. Maureen's hand swiped a clout across her face that was so furious, the room came to a sudden standstill. The bigger shock was that it was Maureen who cried, and not their straight-backed, unmoved young daughter.

'As it's a sin to lie, I believe it's a sort of sin not to trust people as well. If you need to know all my movements, then I'll tell you.' Janet wasn't that sure where she was going to go with this, or how far, and took her time to paint the picture she wanted. Maureen wiped herself back together and went and sat on the other coal box, along the fender, and waited.

'You are not going to like this, and it's my reasoning why I've not mentioned much. I have *never* lied to you; I just kept some things to myself. Right. I go every Sunday to Trafalgar Square. I meet friends who are students there, and they tell me about the Bomb. They march and everything, and I think they are right in what they say, and all this is about me wanting to go to a place called Aldermaston and march back to London, to stop the Bomb.'

'You want to do what? That's what your haircut has all been about, is it? They're Communists, you silly little cow. The police know everything about them, watch them and what not. You'll end up in prison. It's not some game.' Maureen was fizzing with nerves.

'Some bloke has got you into all this, hasn't he?' William thought he was now putting together all the right pieces.

Janet made them sweat a bit longer. She was revelling in the exoticness, and the management of her story. 'If what you mean by that a "boyfriend", then, no, I don't have a "boyfriend". My best friend there is a Dutch bloke called Ben. He is very important in the marches, organizes stuff and that. If you're worried about it, I can bring him here and you can see for yourself. I'm not clever enough for him to fancy me anyway. Those types only go out with each other.'

Maureen didn't like any of it, and was uncomfortable with Janet's couldn't-care-less attitude, but felt at least that they had got some measure of what had been going on. William, on the other hand, was certain there was more. He had seen things that very night, things that didn't quite make a complete set of anything.

'And what makes you late home from work, then?' he asked her.

'Well, sometimes I do actually work a bit later, if there is a lot going on... and sometimes... because Ben might be working late himself, his art college is only down the road from me at Holborn, we meet up for a chat and that. What am I supposed to have done? Blooming hell, anyone would think I've run off with a darkie or something.'

'First things first. No more of this Ban the Bombing lark, we're not having any of that in this house. And now I want some food, I'm fucking starving. You can go and get two lots of fish and chips while I have a word with your mother.'

Chapter Thirty-One

1963 | APRIL

Ivy woke up fully dressed, still wrapped in her beaver lamb coat, with bouncing eyeballs and a brick in her head. It was quarter to nine and she was very late. The half-bottle of cherry brandy on the floor was corkless and empty.

She straightened herself out in the bathroom as lively as she could, swabbing her face with a large dobbet of Pond's Cold Cream to remove yesterday's pancake and mascara. Her lipstick had been completely chewed off during the night. Teeth given a quick once-over and fresh greasepaint applied in seconds. There wasn't much she could do about the crumpling of her blouse and costume, and her hair was much worse, facing this way and that.

The hope had been to get into work before everybody else, maybe have a chance to level things out with Arthur, and take the sting out of yesterday's drama. Ivy's head was throbbing, teeth sweating with nausea, and she felt close to wobbling over and being sick. It more than crossed her mind to take the whole day off, but that would make an appearance on Wednesday even more tricky.

Satanic clouds hovered above her. A taxicab was the only option.

'Good morning, Mr Bertram. Getting warmer, I believe.' Tiny Ivy Brown sashayed as best she could past the front desk and into the lift before the commissionaire had any hope of sucking back into place his top set of dentures in time.

One pig's trotter foot out of the lift and Miss Armstrong was on her. 'Oh, Mrs Brown. Good morning. Are you alright? We were expecting a phone call to say you were poorly or something.' Miss Armstrong looked up at the clock above the lift and moved off.

Ivy also looked up. Quarter to ten. Forty-five minutes late.

To the cloakroom to reorganize herself and hang up the marvel. And now the self-conscious walk through the typing pool to her cubbyhole. It was a long walk from the door to the desk at the end of row five. The clack of her black patent court shoes crashed through the tap-tap-tap of business and stopped everything.

The twenty-four young typists made absolutely no pretence of not ogling her, giving her the once-over, priggishly swanning their necks to follow her quick march through them. A wicked heat of banishment and hatred burned through Ivy. She made a little show of fiddling under her desk, as if arranging places for her handbag, gloves and scarf, but it was the wave of nausea that was keeping her down there. She had no alternative. Feebly, delicately, she spewed into the wastepaper bin.

She shoved sheets of inky carbon paper, copying paper, and torn pages from the notepad into the bin to smother the smell. This was then sprinkled with half a bottle of Flair by Yardley eau de cologne.

The rest of the morning went by almost without incident.

Apart, that is, from the queer mishap with the tea lady and the hot tea. A whole cupful all over the desk, typewriter, letters, the lot. Everything had to be done again. And not even a replacement refreshment or an apology. Another attention-grabbing episode that Ivy could well have done without.

She had written a note addressed to Arthur, in a sealed envelope. If there was no sign of him at lunchtime, the plan was go down to Luderman's in the basement and leave it on the desk.

'Mrs Brown? If you would kindly step this way.' Miss Armstrong had nabbed her before she could get to the cloakroom and out of the building.

Ivy was ushered into the tiny office, attached to Mr Jacob's by a glass door. Windows faced out on to the typing pool, giving the audience of young women out there front row seats.

'Terribly sorry about the time this morning, Miss Armstrong, but I shouldn't really be here. I must have eaten something that's upset my system. I've been violently sick all night.' She quietly urged for sympathy, clutching her handbag, scarf and gloves.

Valerie Armstrong was taking her time. She sat behind her desk and relished every second of leaving Ivy standing there in front of her.

'In fact, if you don't mind, I think it would be for the best if I went home now.'

Miss Armstrong didn't take her eyes off Ivy for a second. Uncertainty lingered in the room. Finally, 'Yes, I agree. I think it would be "for the best" if you went home.'

'Oh thank you. I'm sure I'll be much better by tomorrow. I'll stay late if I have to catch up on anything.' Ivy gave a little nod of polite thanks and turned to leave.

The words pierced her back. 'When I told you to go home, unless I'm much mistaken, I never mentioned your return, did I?'

The whole typing pool witnessed the ginger one's face go into a deathly shock; witnessed her turn back into the room for more. Miss Armstrong, calm and frigid, measured her account with spiteful precision. 'Whenever we enter and exit this building, Mrs Brown, we carry with us the respect and good name of Wiseman Pulverizer Company. Your display… conduct… outside last evening was disgraceful. Mr Bertram in reception was inches from calling the police, apparently.'

Ivy wasn't going to give in easily. She pondered the self-righteous route of indignation, but inched towards something else instead. 'I don't think my personal life has got anything to do with you, if you don't mind my saying so.'

Miss Armstrong smiled out from a tiny corner of her mouth and curled her lip. 'Oh, I'm afraid it does. Especially when it affects other employees and other companies within this building. Mr Bertram said the young man from Luderman's was attacked and barracked out of nowhere by you, and when young Miss Brady tried to calm things down, you got hysterical. He also said that people were stopping in the street to get a good look at the circus you, and you alone, had created.'

Nice, nice, nice Janet Brady, and that stiff-necked pigeon in his overdone ornamental uniform. Ivy watched her world, again, go off into someone else's corner.

She couldn't help herself. Her toenails clawed at the inside of her shoes, her mouth opened the passage to demons. 'Have you any idea how we were all affected when you spent the night here with Mr Jacobs? Some of those girls out there were quite sick at the very thought of it, the two of you together. But I suppose canoodling with the boss doesn't really count as shitting on the "good name of the company", probably got yourself a promotion.'

Valerie Armstrong was bubbling over with pop-eyed terror and humiliation. Ivy Brown looked through the glass into the typing pool and smiled. She had made sure that her final speech was delivered at full throttle. Not angry, but a loud sneer.

'I'll go and collect my cards from Accounts now, shall I?' And with that she sauntered towards the cloakroom for her coat. From behind her she heard a gaggle of typists running to Miss Armstrong's assistance.

Arthur's van wasn't in the backyard. The letter was handed to an ink-splattered old boy taking a heavy carton down to the basement.

Chapter Thirty-Two

1963 | APRIL

That Tuesday afternoon, the typing pool had been poleaxed into quivering silence. Raised eyebrows, peerings over spectacles, and the odd silently mouthed 'What?' flitted across the desks, but no one actually dared make a sound. Miss Armstrong stayed in her office for the rest of the working day, with her pale-green Venetian blinds pulled all the way down and smacked firmly shut.

Lunchtime had been so outrageous that the girls couldn't, or wouldn't, summon up the courage to chance a meet-up and have a pow-wow in the cloakroom.

They watched Eileen take in a second cup of tea (unheard of), with a packet of aspirins, and tried to catch her eye to find out if any further dramas had occurred. Although Miss Armstrong's office had been completely sealed off from peeping Toms, it didn't unclench the grip of her radar, still scouring and exploring the contents of the entire building. At least, that's what it felt like to all beyond her barricade, as if their every breath was even now being monitored by her. The usual five-thirty rush for the exit was performed this night in a funereal hush, tiptoeing around the fallen one.

'Goodnight, ladies, no more turbulence this evening, we hope.'

'And good night to you, Mr Bertram. No. No more turbulence,' Imogen, who was engaged to Piers, said to him. The commissionaire heard faint titters coming from the others, but decided to leave it there. The girls scurried off to the corner of High Holborn, ready to disperse to their different journeys home.

'Oh, come on. Let's brave the pub and have a gab. I've been near to bursting since lunchtime,' Imogen said to them. They shuffled about, looked around to see if Miss Armstrong was on to them, and were tempted both ways: to get out of there as fast as possible, or to go and have a post mortem in the pub. After a lot of umming and aahing, looking at watches, it was decided that Friday night would be the best time. They would wait and see if any more scandals unfolded in the next two days.

Imogen had become the natural leader of the typing pool ever since her arrival three years ago. She had taken her God-given place, completely unaware of her coup, ousting Brenda, the sturdy-looking Feltham girl, who was now relegated to the fringes of the group. About ten of the young women, and Ivy had been one of them, declined any attempt at inclusion in Imogen's orbit, and kept themselves to themselves. But the other fourteen acolytes couldn't wait for what the rest of the week might bring, and the perils of the pub date on Friday; young women in a city pub, unaccompanied by men.

A small huddle of the typing pool was still on the corner as Janet came out. She went out of her way to the other side of the street, hoping they wouldn't see her, hoping they weren't having a conflab about last night, and her. Tony the newsagent, closing his shutters for the night, gave a little wink and a wave as she waited at the end of the long bus queue.

Today had been a peculiar day all round. She had needed to talk about Brian, about the row at home last night, but Eileen had spent the day in a flush of anxiety and seemed to want to avoid speaking to anyone, vanishing into the lavatory more times than normal.

Janet caught them whispering at the bottom of the back stairs, late that afternoon, as Eileen was finishing work. As soon as Eileen had disappeared, Brian lingered just long enough to quietly murmur up to her that Ivy had been sacked and wouldn't be coming back. And that he would explain more in the morning.

It had been impossible, with all the pushing and shoving, even to attempt getting on the first two buses, and this one was so full that Janet had to stand wedged near the platform and the conductor.

'He is *my* tomcat... and he thinks he's moved on to someone else's saucer of milk... someone else's bedroom. But not for long, my dear.' It took Janet a moment to realize that the whisper was meant for her. She turned as the bus came to a stop, and she watched Ivy, in *that* coat, hop off the bus and march back down towards the office. Where had she come from? There had been no sign of her before. Was she following her?

That Thursday morning, the weather was feeling and smelling more like April. Easter just around the corner, end of next week.

Prepared to snap their girdles in their excitement to get to work, most of the girls from the typing pool arrived earlier than usual, to organize themselves and be at their desks, ready for action, before any complaint could come from a more than unpredictable Miss Armstrong.

Prurience was in the air.

Miss Armstrong was not.

The sniggering was at the phone call. To Mr Jacobs himself, perhaps?

Anyway, they were told the news by Widow Twankey, Mrs Freda Bailey, private secretary to the big boss upstairs, 'part-timer Jensen'. Jensen was a two-days-a-week man, and most of the staff queried, quite often, what old widow Bailey did up there to occupy her time and earn her keep.

'Owing to a bout of nervous exhaustion, Miss Armstrong will not be returning to work this week. It is possible, and hoped for, that she will find herself fit enough to resume her normal duties on Monday. Any problems, you report directly to me. Thank you, ladies.'

It was obvious to all that Mrs Bailey had hated being the deliverer of such potential titillation. She squirmed out, with her beaky nose leading the way, as proudly as she could. Valerie Armstrong and Freda Bailey had never been close.

It was only by the time Eileen came round with morning tea that any of them realized that Mr Jacobs was also unavailable for work that day. They had watched as Eileen tapped on his door and walked in to a deserted room and empty desk. Over lunchtime, the girls decided that the pub gathering should happen that very night.

Chapter Thirty-Three

1963 | APRIL

T hat Saturday had been one of Janet's longest days, most of it spent in her bedroom, refusing Katherine her rightful share of it until bedtime. Janet stared at the ceiling as it changed from the dungeon of night to bright Sunday morning. How to get out of the house?

Her week had been a mixture of everything. To get through it, with careful tugs at the reins of freedom, had required some stealth. Muddling up home times seemed to be a good start. Tuesday night, home at the usual, almost to the second. Wednesday, chanced being ten minutes behind schedule, and got away with it. Thursday and Friday, really pushed the boat out, and got a lift home in the van with Brian. Right outside her front door. If anyone saw, it was never mentioned.

Janet crept to the bathroom, thinking the whole household was still fast asleep, and was surprised to see Maureen and the littlies already dressed and ready for early morning Mass.

'And why are you up so sprightly and hovering about this morning?' Maureen asked.

'Mum! I'm going to the toilet. I was trying not to wake anybody.'

'Right. Well, as your father's told you, there'll be no galli-vanting today. I'll be back in an hour and then you can help with the veg.' Maureen slipped out with the toddlers as quietly as possible, using her key to close the front door.

Janet didn't have a plan as such, but thought it best to be washed, dressed, and ready for anything. Half an hour later, she was in the kitchen, concentrating out of the window, when there was movement and someone else attacked the bathroom. Over the sound of a bath running, she heard the echoing double cough of her father. Janet concerned herself with the peeling of potatoes. She was on to washing the leaves of a large cabbage when William filled the door frame of the kitchen. He was standing there, freshly shaven, in his white singlet, best suit trousers and socks.

'Has your mother gone to church?' he said.

Janet didn't look at him, nodded, and carried on with the cabbage.

William Brady scrutinized this new-fangled invention in front of him, covered from head to toe in black. Sixteen years old and choosing widow's weeds. Black roll-neck sweater, tight black pants, flat black pumps. Her lovely innocent hair, butchered into this docked cap of revolution. Her uniform of dissent.

'I could do with a cup of tea and a bit of toast. Put the kettle on.' He went back to the bedroom.

All Janet could think about was how to get out of the house. Potatoes, cabbage and carrots had been peeled, washed and put into their separate saucepans by the time William came down for his breakfast. He was all spruced up in his navy suit. His only suit. Grey tie, polished black shoes, and a peek of blue silk just nosing out of his breast pocket. He might have been ready for a wedding, but his face had the grim mask of a coffin-carrier about it. He kept looking at his watch.

'Look at the pair of us, Dad. All dressed up and nowhere to go.' She used her nan's favourite comment, trying to break the awkward gloom.

'I'm dressed up with somewhere very important to go. You, young lady, are going nowhere but here. Mark my words, me and your mother mean it.' His tone orphaned her, separated her.

William took another check at his watch, slurped the dregs of his tea, gave Janet a curious stare, and left the house.

Trafalgar Square was almost empty at that time on a Sunday morning. When William had left the house, she'd waited a good fifteen minutes before chancing her escape. Maureen and the littlies could get back any moment. The teeth-clamping tension didn't ease off until the bus was halfway to the Strand. The pigeons were up and swooping around a potty-looking old girl covered in breadcrumbs.

Janet dawdled, killing time.

She crossed between the fountains and watched the elderly specimen joyfully fling up and out lumps of white bread, every now and then digging into an ancient, low-lying pram that was stuffed with newspapers, a pile of grubby-looking clothes, and about ten different-sized bags and holdalls. It was trembling under the weight. Hanging off the handle were some blue Christmas tinsel, blowing in the breeze, a wrinkly orange balloon, and, dangling on two large butcher's hooks, a rusty frying pan and a metal egg-slice. Beneath the grime and detritus, there were signs that the pram had once been a baby cream colour.

Janet sat on the edge of the fountain. Sprinkles of water pattered on to the shoulders of her coat; the coat that reminded her of schooldays, childhood. She'd had her eye on it, displayed in Marshall's front window, ever since Maureen had told her that they would buy her a new outfit ready for leaving school and starting work. She had been so proud of it in the beginning. Now, all she longed for was a short, dark brown duffel coat, with real bone toggles. Marshall's of Aldgate wouldn't possess a duffel like that. No call for it in that neck of the woods. Everyone there wanted a version of this grey lady's overcoat, knee-length, suit-styled lapels, two waist pockets, and the real fashion marker, the half-belt at the back.

The pigeon lady was prancing around the fountain with birds perched on her arms, her shoulders, and one hopping about on her head, fighting to stay on. She was coming towards Janet, raving in a blissful euphoria; doll-like, with white-powdered face, little pink circles of rouge in the middle of her cheeks, and poppy-coloured lips painted into a sharp bow. Her head was wrapped in three separate wool scarves, knotted at the front into turbans. Grey hair, corrugated into two skinny plaits, poked out beneath this crown of black, yellow and blue. Knots and scarf tassels skew-whiffed this way and that. Yellow and black liquid oozed down the slalom; bird shit stopping short of reaching her face, breached by each knot. The pigeon then flew off and preened itself at the feet of Lord Nelson.

The old lady's clothes, if they could be referred to as

clothes, were a magician's jamboree: a down-to-the-ankles purple velvet dress, overlaid with a pinky flattened tutu reaching her knees, two wide leather belts around her skinny waist. Piled on top of this was a dark fur jacket, brooches pinned all over her, dangly diamanté earrings, and what seemed like hundreds of thin Indian bracelets clanking around her wrists. A whirling dervish of Bedlam.

There were the beginnings of a few stragglers coming into the square: a few men with their newspapers, searching for somewhere to perch and read, and a couple of others just passing through, making a wide berth to avoid the pigeon woman.

'St Francis of Assisi, St Francis of Assisi, here, in old London town. They love me. Me. These magnificent creatures of God.' She had a tiny delicate voice. Twirling around, her arms windmilling, she was getting closer and closer to Janet. Big Ben struck ten laborious chimes.

The ancient doll came to a sudden full stop, quivering with timid excitement. Listening for something, her ears cocked to the side, it was as if she were waiting for a delayed gong.

'Did he ask for me, dear? My name? Did he ask for Mildred, Mildred Courtney?' Her genteel manner and lady-like tone blurred the riches-to-rags image.

'Pardon?' Janet said.

A flash of spite flew across the antique painted face. She rubbed her hands together, the fingerless gloves revealing filthy fingernails and chipped red nail varnish. She pushed her whispering face very close. 'Are *you* called Mildred? Are you? No. No, dear, you're not. Can you fly? No, dear, you can't. But don't pretend you didn't hear my name. I'm always the first to be called. The first to be called.'

167

Janet squirmed her way to an upright position and wriggled out of potential harm's way. She crossed the square and walked up the steps to the main road. Only when she was far enough away did she turn back and look. The old girl was gabbling to the exact spot as if Janet were still sitting there.

A few minutes past ten. Brian wouldn't be arriving until three. Thoughts of later on, and returning home, kept filtering through. Half-resolved plots of excuses couldn't take away the facts of the matter. She was in deep trouble. Janet sat on the wall outside the National Gallery and stared down Whitehall towards Big Ben. She was hungry, thirsty, and miserable.

More and more people were swarming around, into the square, and through the revolving doors of the gallery behind her. She went on the hunt for chocolate.

Chapter Thirty-Four

1963 | APRIL

These feelings were second nature to her. No panic. But it would take some time to fathom out which, and what, punishment. Ivy's narrow spirit was pleasured and fed by the idea that, because of her, other lives could be altered for ever. Miss Armstrong's tumble from her perch had kept Ivy amused all week: a public tumble that would be almost impossible to recover from.

'Oh my God, Ivy, you're still here? Haven't you gone home at all?' Pandora kicked the door shut and let go of everything. Her bright orange coat, two magazines, and a small suitcase fell at her feet.

'No,' was all she could come up with.

'Coffee. I need coffee. I'm bloody exhausted and really pissed off.'

Ivy put the kettle on and went to clear up the abandoned belongings by the door.

'Do you have any intentions, ever, of leaving?' Pandora stared out of the French window, her long legs dangling over the side of the armchair.

'Depends.' Ivy shoved the suitcase and coat into the bedroom and sauntered back to the kettle. No more was said between them until the coffee appeared.

'I've had a fucking, fucking, horrible, grisly three days. You cannot imagine. I don't think I'm ever going home again. They can fuck themselves. When they do finally pop their clogs, my nasty squealy little bruv is going to inherit everything. Everything.'

She had seen Pandora in various combinations of drama and fury, but this was different. This was nearly tears. Ivy chanced her first move. 'I've cleaned the place up, and done any washing I found, so you have all clean clothes… and I enjoyed it… I surprised myself actually. I don't know if you remember, I did mention it, but I left my job on Tuesday… and what I was thinking…'

'Please, Ivy, please get to the point. I'm in no mood for yokel ramblings right at the moment. I have spent the last three evenings at my father's bloody *drugless* house and supper table, stuck to a greasy, tawdry Tory MP, and with nothing more than a few glasses of wine to soften the view.'

'No, it doesn't matter. I'll talk to you about it another time, maybe.'

'I'm sorry, honey, I'm being an absolute cunt. Move on.' She clamped her coffee cup with both hands and gave Ivy a sweet wink that reeked of asking forgiveness.

'I wondered if you would like me to look after you. Girl Friday, that sort of thing, with cleaner and general housekeeper thrown in. If I lived in, I wouldn't charge much.'

Pandora blinked in disbelief, and horror, knowing for the life of her that it would be a disaster, although a crumb of temptation dangled there. Ivy waited for this new concoction of her life.

Pandora unsprawled herself and carefully, submissively, knelt in front of Ivy, who was leaning against the window. 'I have to ask you this. Are you telling me... in your roundabout way... you are in love with me?'

The plan was hatching out of its bounds, and Ivy needed time to figure out the best of the only two possible answers. 'Um. I don't think that's got anything to do with it, actually. Not to my mind.'

'Ivy, listen to me. You mustn't love me. I think you are... sweet... and... a very interesting person, really, but I can't love anybody. Okay? This is not about you, it's about me. Now, I think before we come to any grief you should get your things. We'll go down... What time is it?... Yes, down to the pub, have some lunch and a few drinks, my treat, and leave it at that.'

Pandora was still in the praying position, waiting for an answer, when Ivy's knee shot out and crunched into her face, savagely flinging her backwards with such force it knocked the armchair over. For a few seconds, Ivy stared down into her enemy, scanning the broken nose, the blood and mess she had created in that flash, then calmly moved off, rubbing her sore knee, into the bathroom and bedroom to collect her possessions.

At the door she took one last look around the room. Pandora hadn't moved much, but was now lying curled up in her own embrace of comfort.

Chapter Thirty-Five

1963| APRIL

'Left already? Why so early?' Rosa had her feet in a bowl of soapy hot water, and in front of her, on the kitchen table, were the torture accoutrements of chiropody.

'It's all my fault, Mum, I told her that if Sunday dinner couldn't be ready by one o'clock, then count me out. I've got to be somewhere.' Brian fluttered his eyelashes at Rosa, and grinned the grin of the smitten.

'I bet she didn't have any breakfast. I don't know why she don't stop this Mrs Clarke palaver. I think it's depressing her. Don't you reckon?' She threw a glance at him to see if he'd noticed anything, or knew something that she didn't.

Standing in front of the ironing board in his pale blue Y-fronts and grey socks, Brian carried on pressing the black drainpipe trousers, carefully dampening one of Albert's large handkerchiefs in a pudding basin ready for the heat and fume of the iron.

'She promised to be back by eleven, and I've got to warm the oven at quarter to,' Brian said.

The piercing swoop and crackle of wireless tuning came from the front room. Albert was searching for some cheerful Sunday ragtime, anything other than the morning service.

'Albert, turn it in, for Christ's sake, I can't hear myself think in here.' Rosa's shout was muffled by heavy banging on the neighbour's front door below. Albert persevered with his aggravating twiddling: the wireless crossing continents, unknown languages fighting with each other for airspace, and every now and again a scrap of holy choir or the intoning misery of an English sermon. He finally surrendered, switched it off, and went to the lavatory with the *News of the World*. Brian added more hot water to Rosa's feet from the kettle and continued with the ironing. Now on to his white shirt with fancy button-down collar.

A mumble of voices could just about be deciphered coming from downstairs, and then their door buzzer went. 'Ignore it. It's probably the Jehovah's,' Rosa said.

'If I was decent and had some trousers on, I'd go and tell them to piss off, say I'm Jewish.'

The buzz came again and again, harder and longer each time. Brian, in an incensed spin, rushed down and flung open the street door. A man and his finger were glued to the buzzer.

'Oi, what do you think you're doing?' He pulled the man's arm away.

William Brady gave Brian a good look over. Taking his time. He had no intention of humiliating himself, and needed to keep the situation, whatever it might be, under some sort of control.

'I'm sorry. I didn't mean to wake you up. I need to talk to you about my daughter. Can I come inside?' This didn't sound like a request. It was said in a flat, cold 'I have a search warrant' manner of a police constable, someone who held all the cards.

Brian was showing the street his underpants and gammy leg. That fragile, undernourished twin to his good leg. He was in a quandary. And his silence convinced William Brady there was something unsavoury going on.

'I'm talking about my daughter Janet. Don't try and deny anything, because I've been following you. How do you think I knew where you live?'

'Janet? Following me? What for? What am I supposed to have done? Is she alright?'

'I just want a quiet word, and I would much prefer if it wasn't out here.'

Brian didn't exactly let him in, but before he knew it he was indicating the way upstairs, following quickly up the rear.

'What's happened to her… please tell me she's alright.' He took William into the front room, his heart pounding with grimness and the possible horror to come.

With Rosa trapped in her bowl in the kitchen, he hoped that Albert would stay in the lavatory until the newspaper had been read cover to cover. He needed to cope with whatever was coming alone.

'Who is it, Bri?' Rosa shouted out.

'It's alright, Mum, it's something to do with work. It's a workmate… You're frightening me, mate, please tell me what's going on.'

William gave a few seconds to the thought that maybe what he had to say would be best said in front of the young man's parents, but he needed to make this as small and straightforward a drama as possible, and to get on with it.

'The last thing I want to do is cause any upset, so I'll get straight to the point, and leave you and your family in peace. I'm sure you're just a normal young bloke and all that, but, I don't know if you're aware of this, our daughter is only just sixteen. Sixteen. And she should be mixing with friends her own age. Me and her mother don't reckon it's healthy that a man of your age should be playing around with a kid. I don't mean to be rude. You ought to be with a grown woman, thinking about settling down and that.'

Brian bunged the laughter in. The relief that it was only this. He knew in that moment he had to keep William on his side, and not let him get the better of him. 'You scared the life out of me there for a minute. Do you mind if I get some trousers on? I don't know how old you think I am. I'm twenty-two. You make me sound like a dirty old man.'

They were both so focused on each other that they didn't hear Rosa pad in. Facing the door, William saw her first. The blood drained from his face. Without taking her eyes off the stranger in her front room, she said, 'Brian, what's going on?'

'I'm not sure, Mum, just leave us be for a mo, go back into the kitchen. Go on.'

Rosa sniffed a conspiracy that was being kept from her. She scrutinized the complete stamp of this unasked-for visitor. William, within his breath-held silence, was a few steps ahead of her. A bigger reckoning than he had allowed for was unfolding before him.

The tight, shy, bum-clenching awkwardness from the three of them collapsed into a paralysed hush. Rosa's conspiracy, of her own making, from all those years ago, had returned home. The gloom that slowly descends before an uncalled-for, unwanted surprise seeped into the room. A chain was pulled in the background, and the murmur of slippers and rustle of newspaper moved towards the living room.

'Mum? Did you call her Mum?' William's shallow breathing could barely support the words.

Albert, already humpy, found something very peculiar was happening to his Sunday morning and he didn't like the look of any of it.

William's flesh slacked off his bones. He took a snap in his mind's eye of the three people before him. Old Rosa, fearful and lost. Albert trying to keep up, vacillating between being well pissed off with this morning's events and needing to get to the bottom of them. Then Brian, standing there in his underpants and socks, looking half-finished, somehow not completely coloured in. William needed a bit more before he jumped the gun, but Rosa had rearranged herself the quickest and was scouting around for a safety net.

'Brian. Upstairs. Upstairs, I said. Now move.'

Brian wasn't going anywhere; trapped in his own bafflement, watching the spectacle of his mother cooking herself up into a right old sweat. Nothing too urgent was occurring to Albert, other than in his own home some stranger was ruling the roost. Rosa was dizzy with a manic queerness. Her eyes darting this way and that, she grabbed William by the arms and tried to pummel him out of the door. 'Out! Out now, and keep your fucking gob shut or I'll shred your tongue myself.' She was building to a pitch. She kept looking and listening out for Eileen.

'Oi, oi, oi! What's the matter with you, woman. Calm down.

Who is he? What you up to, chum?' Albert peeled her away, gave her to Brian, who sat her down in the armchair.

She was done for.

Chapter Thirty-Six

1963 | APRIL

Janet was rescued by Ben at around midday and taken off for an under-age drink and a bag of crisps in the pub. He had been surprised to find her at the gallery that early, but she wouldn't give anything away. These Sundays, in the sparkle of the city, helped her breathe in a new universe, if only for an afternoon. The first sip of lemonade shandy made her tongue yawn and poke out, gagging for air. Janet said it tasted like the inside of a tin can and would have prefered a cream soda. Ben lisped and Dutched his peculiar English around his timetable: the arrangements made for the upcoming Easter March; when that was over, a few days back in Holland with his family; then he would do this and then that. All energy, plans, and glorious freedom; in his theatre he could play any part he wanted, when he wanted. Janet knew, even though in the right costume, that most of her was still hovering in the wings, with one tiny toe poking out on to the stage. But the curtain could go up at any minute. And she wanted to be ready.

The slow clock of the morning had taken a bit of a spurt

since Ben had turned up. Trafalgar Square and the surrounding streets were filling up with Londoners and tourists from the suburbs, who were gradually emerging from their near-hibernation of that vile winter.

They had gone for a walk, up and behind the gallery. Crossing the road towards the Coliseum Theatre, he showed her this dirty, scary alley, too narrow for any hope of side-by-side walking. Ben went ahead and almost three-quarters of the way down he pointed to a door. The secret door, he said, where, late in the evenings, only men were allowed; an illegal door. Janet couldn't grasp what he was implying. Ben laughed at her ignorance, grabbed the palm of her hand and kissed it.

'If ever you are in trouble, you know, I have a place for you,' he said.

'Thank you.'

'Why don't you stay in my flat when I go back to the Nederlands? You too can be the burglar alarm, for me this time.'

'Thank you, I might.'

It was three o'clock before she knew it. Ben sat and waited with her, on the wall outside the gallery, where Brian would know to find her.

'When do you stop being frightened of your parents?'

'When you stop bothering to lie to them, and they get to know who you really are.' Ben made it sound so straightforward.

But she wasn't sure that she wanted them to know who she really was. Not quite yet.

'You know? I am as lonely as you. As lost, some days, as you. But we have to live, and be good people. That's all you can try and do. This big drama you won't speak about, it's not good, stuck there inside you,' Ben said.

Janet had taken a dangerous leap today.

Brian had promised he would go back home with her. Convince them all of his love and care, that he would make everything alright.

But he never came. The crushing battles of heartbreak and terror embalmed and suffocated her. She was too young and immortal to have the grown-up imaginings of accidents and deaths. Brian had abandoned her, no excuses.

On the top of the bus, she shilly-shallied over her diminishing options. Go home, or go to the address in Wapping that Ben had scribbled down, where he would be at a meeting that night.

About half a dozen stops before her own, Janet got off the bus. It was five o'clock and just beginning to lose the light. She trudged the long, roundabout way to home, the familiar streets, buildings, people, everything she had known since childhood, looking faintly sinister, as if they had already thrown her out and orphaned her.

Janet didn't use her key. She knocked on the door like an unwanted caller, a visitor.

It wasn't the reception she had prepared herself for. Both William and Maureen answered the door together. Maureen grabbed her first, hugging her and mewling gently. William softly eased the front door shut, took Janet by the hand and walked them both into the front room. The flat was empty of everyone else. No littlies running harum-scarum, no Katherine to give her the nods up and a bit of support. The weird atmosphere paralysed everything that had already happened to her that day.

William pulled out two of the dining chairs from the table, put them in the middle of the room, and sat Janet down, and then himself, facing her. Maureen went to the armchair at the fireside and curled into it. Hiding.

'Now, Janet. I'm not angry, but I need the truth. No lies, okay?' William said.

She stared right through him, sitting upright, not moving.

'Ask her. For Christ's sake, ask her.' Maureen shouted into the fire. 'Let's get this over and done with.'

Janet wasn't going to help them. She would answer only what was required.

'I know you didn't meet that bloke this morning… we'll come to that later… but did you see him at all today?' he said.

'No.'

William braced himself. The next bit could go tits up, and he needed to keep hold of his authority and some sense of delicacy.

'I know that you have already kissed him, because I've seen it with my own eyes.' He eyed her for some reaction.

Janet looked into the skin and pores of her father's face, and saw his planned future for her. Why were men given the world to see, but girls, women, were allowed just a few close streets? A life to be lived only a mile long, she thought. She felt dizzy, her eyes hard as marbles, working so hard to be a near-invisible wraith. Janet watched the walls of the living room collapse into the bedrooms, the bedroom walls collapse into the street, and she could see streets and roads stretching into the mist.

'Oh my life… what's going on. Pick her up, pick her up.' Maureen scrambled from the armchair.

William lifted Janet on to the sofa and undid the top buttons of her coat.

'Get a glass of water and a couple of cream crackers. I bet she's not eaten all bloody day,' Maureen said, squidging on to the edge of the sofa and patting some life back into her daughter's cold hands.

Not that many days ago, William and Maureen had set about an everyday journey of keeping a protective eye on one of their kids. Had it really all started over a haircut? Janet munched on the cracker, wondering what she could have done to have to live through a day like this one. The cracker was relentlessly masticated into a swelling pulp that made it impossible to swallow and almost choked her. Maureen rushed her into the bathroom. They stayed in there together longer than suited William. He was travelling his words every which way, how best to say just enough and no more.

'Talk to me, Jan. Come on, and Mum will make it all right, I promise. Tell me what's going on and I'll deal with Dad.' Janet sat on the side of the bath and watched the red and green steam-proof wallpaper. That particular red bolted together with that particular green created, if you stared hard enough, a brutal optical illusion: a clash and jump of colours flickering like an ancient peep show, an eyeball game she had played in there since schooldays.

Brian's abandonment had altered everything and weighed her down with new-found years. Her heart stopped lurching, she was filling up with a quietness she had never experienced before.

'I don't want to go back to work. Ever again. If you make me, I still won't go. I can't.' And with that she got up and returned to whatever William felt like throwing at her. Behind her back, Maureen gave him a glad-eye nod.

'We can make the best of this, Will. She decided herself. She doesn't want to go back to that job anyway. I've not said a word.'

But that wasn't the end of it for him. His imagination had stepped up a few more notches than Maureen's. 'No lies now. Has that bloke touched you? Been where he shouldn't with you?'

*

'You should have heard them. Mum was screaming and crying, then walloped him, I heard a great tussle. I was really frightened at one point. That's when Dad chucked me and the littlies out, and told us to go to Nan's.' Katherine was whispering with scandal, and trying to clamber into Janet's bed.

She lay trying to block out her sister's excitement and theatrics. All this fuss over nothing. A no-longer boyfriend... the inappropriate, not good enough boyfriend, who had pissed off anyway. She thought about tomorrow morning, and what stories or gossip when she didn't turn up. What would Eileen think?

Katherine was not going to surrender until it was all out. 'He'd kept it a secret all those years... I still can't believe it. Mum was shouting, "How many more little bastards have you got floating around? And you tell everyone else how to behave, you fucking hypocrite." I was listening to all this in the kitchen and they'd forgotten I was there. Then Dad started crying and calling your name. I thought you'd died or something for a minute.'

It was the 'fucking' that made Janet sit up and take notice. It sounded foreign, a new-fangled shape... position, for

Katherine's mouth to make, something dangerous and very bad. They heard a creeping movement outside in the passage, and knew at any minute the doorknob would turn. Being checked up on. Katherine flattened herself into a sleeping position and gurgled gentle tired sounds. Janet stayed sitting up, daring another interrogation. Through the gloom, towards the tiniest crack in the door, she couldn't tell who the peeking eye belonged to. Whoever it was quickly went away and closed the door. Katherine carefully resurrected herself from under the blankets and lifted her head. Both girls couldn't understand, with Janet sitting there on full alert, why no one dared to enter.

'Anyway… it turns out that Dad has got another kid somewhere else, from some woman during the war. Can you imagine?' Katherine let this out in one full-throttled whisper.

Janet got up, wrapped a blanket round herself, and went to the living room. There were signs that someone had made a bed on the couch, and had now left it. In the midnight chill, she played with the half-finished jigsaw laid out on the sideboard. Jesus had already been filled in, and looked furious, his accusing arms cursing the money-changers. As the grey marbled night shifted slightly into a new dawn, Janet returned to bed. It was five o'clock.

Chapter Thirty-Seven

1963 | APRIL

Above the city of London, the high April sun cracked through racing puffs of huge snowy clouds, its gimlet eye blinding drivers, travellers and walkers alike, battling their way to work. The cold wind blew hats off, skirts and coats were lifted, exposing the odd suspender and mottled pink skin just below knickers, or trapped and stuck between legs, making it hobblingly difficult to walk. Street detritus of paper and cardboard swirled and eddied across the wide main streets, making it a Grand National hurdle for cyclists. The Blitz spirit that had got Londoners through the hell of winter was now waning and returning them to their closed-off, 'mind your own beeswax' private world.

This Monday morning's sneak preview of spring could be seen all over the place. From newsagents to hairdressers, almost every shop window displayed Easter eggs. Two shops along from Holborn Tube station, the cobbler's-cum-key cutter's had livened up its usual depressing frontage with a row of Smartie-filled eggs. Plonked in the middle, to break up the line, was a bunch of plastic daffodils in an orange glass vase. If a customer spent more than ten shillings in there, in the next ten days, they would get a free raffle ticket and a chance to win one of the eggs.

In the typing pool at Wiseman Pulverizer, Ivy's desk had a new incumbent, a freshly widowed vicar's wife from Penge, genteel poverty shoving her mature years back to employment; a temp from an overcharging Westminster agency, praying for a permanent booking.

For Eileen, the moment she'd returned from Mrs Clarke's, Sunday and Monday had oozed into each other. Of the many concoctions, over twenty-two years, that had sifted through her, Eileen could never have reckoned on this one.

She'd stayed all night in the armchair by the fire, but Brian never came back. Why wouldn't he wait until she got home? They must have missed each other only by about fifteen minutes. To occupy the madness, crumpled and barely washed, she had left for the office hours early. He would turn up for work, she was sure of that, unless some other disaster smashed into him. Her heart flipped at the thought.

She had spent the morning up and down to the yard, searching for him. Somehow, in a twenty-minute gap, she discovered that his van had slipped out to do the rounds. Should be finished and done with by around half past four, the old boy in the loading bay had told her. When it became obvious that Janet wasn't turning up today, more imagined wreckage floated to the surface.

Janet was allowed to stay in bed for as long as she wanted. 'Please, please, don't let on that I've told you,' were Katherine's last words to her before going off to school.

Maureen could be heard domesticating around the place and dealing with the littlies from time to time. By midday, she suggested it was time for Janet to get washed, dressed, and have something to eat.

She did everything she was told to do, but in complete silence. Janet ate the two boiled eggs and soldiers of bread, tasting nothing, all the while chewing on the escape plan. Things had slid overnight from heartbreak to mayhem. Eileen would be the only one to be able to tell the everything of it, so she would have to get to Wiseman's before four thirty. But even more urgently, before William got back.

At two o'clock, as the toddlers were being changed and fed, Janet crawled and inched her way down the long passage, grabbed her coat off the hook, and ran, leaving the street door wide open. The weather didn't occur to her until she was in it.

Chapter Thirty-Eight

1963 | April

Ivy lay flat on her back on the little bed. She held a lollipop-shaped hand mirror above her and examined her face. Now that she didn't have to pass muster with Miss Armstrong any more, her make-up was a little heavier than usual. Her hated ginger freckles had been almost completely erased by ivory pancake, a brown pencil had filled in eyebrows and drawn a flick-up line above her eyelids. Brown block mascara was then spat, licked, and brushed on albino eyelashes. Salmon-pink lipstick smudged well beyond the tiny crack of a mouth. She smiled at herself, revealing the tiny fence of teeth. This carefully applied artwork, meant to disguise her natural colouring, had unfortunately done the opposite. On top of that, the pancake and powder brushed up the fine hairs on her downy face, giving her the look of an over-furry apricot.

The sudden crash of a heavy downpour outside turned Ivy's prone body towards the window. She chewed over her options, as rain bashed the glass panes. A movement forward was the obvious need. A change, an alteration in the scheme of things for everyone, because she would not suffer this alone. It was the only way that Ivy, from as far back as she could remember, knew how to operate. It was the pulse and wattage of her: outrages and slights, portioned out to the innocent to dilute her own agony.

The moment of attack and its geography, for getting the maximum effect, ruminated through her. It was ten o'clock in the morning, and the one thing she was absolutely sure of was that it would occur some time that afternoon.

There were many hours to fill until then.

Chapter Thirty-Nine

1963 | APRIL

Fred decided, with the pair of them not having slept much, that he was in the better state to do the driving. The traffic wasn't too bad, but everything would take a bit longer than usual, as Fred and his dodgy eyesight went at a more sedate pace. Halfway through the morning the heavens opened and they crawled almost to a standstill, windscreen wipers working overtime and scratching at the glass. Brian faced out the window, seeing nothing, and couldn't think of a word to utter.

'I'm going to pull over in a minute and take a break. Gasping for a cuppa,' Fred said, as he manoeuvred the van down a side street opposite Waterloo station. At the sight of a pub, he quickly changed his tune. 'Oh sod it, let's make a dash for it, go for a pint and a pie. I can't see a bloody thing in this and it's giving me a headache.'

Brian had arrived banging on his door yesterday afternoon, already a bit pissed, but coherent enough to give the gist of the day. Yet Fred couldn't quite fathom the cause of such ridiculous excitement. He was touched that Brian had come to him first, but was it all really enough to leave home for?

'I reckon you should eat something with that. Just to be on the safe side,' Fred said, giving Brian's whisky a little nod, at the same time biting into his steaming meat pasty.

'No, I'm fine… not hungry… Might have a bag of crisps in a while.'

The pub had hardly anyone in it, but was bouncing with shouts, the racket coming from a group of about eight on the other side of the horseshoe-shaped bar. 'Actors apparently,' Fred said. 'Actors from that old theatre up the road. That's what the barman tells me, anyhow. I thought I'd brought you to an up-your-bum queer joint. That would have pleased your mother no end.'

'Thought they were the local nutcases,' was all Brian could muster. He threw the tot of whisky down his gullet in one go.

Fred plotted carefully his words of wisdom. His young friend needed a kick up the arse to get going on the right track again. 'What you young people are finding really difficult in this day and age… is… How can I put this without being bloody rude? Well, frankly, Brian… in the end, it's about respect. You kids want everything your own way these days. What happened yesterday was an everyday occurrence in my day. Girls weren't allowed anywhere much without Dad giving his say-so. Good fathers, that is. All you have got to do is… if your heart is really broken over this… get yourself round to his drum and let him know your honourable intentions. Bet your boots you'll come out smelling of roses.'

'You don't know the half of it,' Brian said, and dropped his face to hide tears.

Chapter Forty

1963 | April

The house was quiet, the other lodgers having left for work a couple of hours ago. Ivy decided on a tiptoe around. Turning the handle to the next-door room, it was, as she had thought it would be, locked. And the next. But the room facing her, at the end of the hall, was accessible. Her heart stuttered in case she had made some mistake and the occupant was still in situ.

Ivy whispered a shaky 'Hello?' and got no response. Closing the door she leaned against it and considered the room. It was an absolute tip: clothes all over floor, wardrobe flung open and more clobber spewing and dangling out of that. This room was bigger than her own, with more than enough space for the double bed. At first glance, it was a female room, albeit sluttish and chaotic. The sideboard by the dishevelled, rumpled bed was covered in bathroom paraphernalia of toothbrush and paste, soap, perfume; then tweezers, nail polish, hair curlers, a couple of lipsticks and black mascara, in a narrow lozenge of a box. But the more she poked around, the more confusing the occupant became. A pair of brown brogues, men's, in a size nine, a couple of pairs of grey trousers, men's, a large blazer with some boating motif on the breast pocket. Among these were two pairs of stilettos, a black pair of winkle pickers, and a silver, open-toed pair. The few things that had remained on their hangers were some shimmery ladies' cocktail dresses and a shiny blue kimono.

Bile rose in Ivy's throat. An illicit couple lived here, creeping about, having the life of Riley. The temptation to tell the old bag of a landlady downstairs was volcanic, but second thoughts pumped in, about how to explain the discovery. Ivy decided to bide her time. Get today and all its connotations over with, and then enjoy herself with this nastiness later.

She tried to conjure up the age and class of these tenants. Who had she come across on the stairs, or on the dash to the bathroom? In all the years there, she had only clocked retreating backs, the odd footfall or cough. Forensically, she lifted the bedclothes for signs of orgiastic activity. There were none; none that Ivy could spot, anyway. Flicking through the wardrobe, she fancied around with trying on, and maybe pinching, something. Her arm mid-air, the queerness of this room finally dawned on her. Every shoe was a size nine; all the frocks were man-sized, and a big man at that. Rummaging through the drawer in the sideboard, the only clues to the occupant or occupants were personal papers belonging to a Mr John Clegg. Wage slips showed that he worked for Brownlow Gentleman's Outfitters in Edgware Road.

Back in the safety of her own room, Ivy put the blue diamanté clip earrings she had relieved Mr Clegg of, on the chest of drawers, and propped his huge black umbrella against the wall under the window. 'He'll be more than sorry,' she thought.

There was no let-up from the bludgeoning rain, and it was probably in for the whole day. This afternoon's jaunt was not one for the plastic concertina hat.

She had a count-up of her cash, and what was left in the Post Office savings book. Four pounds and fifteen shillings in the purse, and the grand total of forty-seven pounds and ten shillings saved with the Post Office.

Chapter Forty-One

1963 | APRIL

Eileen, up in her eyrie, dressed and ready for home, wasn't going anywhere until that van returned. It was four-thirty.

Vehicles exited the yard on to the cobbled lane and then out on to Kingsway, but couldn't enter that way, because of the one-way traffic system. They would have to return passing either her window at the front, or the corner one. She flitted constantly between the two, struggling to see through the downpour.

Without taking her eye off the street below, her hands went to the drawer under the sink and felt around for the small, thin packet of five cigarettes. It was her second fag that day. They had been lying in that drawer since the New Year, when the young man from the architects' room, desperate to give up, had asked Eileen to keep them for him in case of an emergency.

She kept telling herself that all this must be for the best. At least he knew the nub of it now. But it didn't take away the terrible gnawing, the possible forever loss of him.

Eileen took long, slow drags on the cigarette and watched as buses and odd bits of traffic ploughed through the deep puddles, three-foot-high sprays drenching the pavements and all who were unfortunate enough to be scurrying by; umbrellas shooting out sideways as shields at the sound of an engine's rumble.

Eileen focused through the dribbling window panes at the people squelching together, down there in shop doorways. But the dead had been resurrected and wouldn't leave her alone. The remembrance of hard-to-come-by wartime rations that Rosa and Albert had shared with young Private Brady all those years ago. Mollycoddling him, and hypnotizing themselves into remaking a semblance of their own shot-down, exploded son.

William Brady. How much she had thought she'd loved him then. William fucking Brady. She had always pictured him a corpse. The light switched off with all the others, somewhere, sometime, in Burma.

By the time Brian was around four years old, the war was over, and the old ache for her soldier had been sieved into the oblivion box. Brian would be Rosa and Albert's feeble compensation for everything. And they had kidnapped him from her. 'All for the best' was their cock-eyed philosophy.

The rain slurped to an abrupt standstill, clouds blew high away, and the sun brilliantly dazzled out, lighting up the city. Umbrellas were furled, doorways were cleared, and, avoiding the perils of the kerbside cascades, people went about their business. Eileen saw the van bend into the main road, and watched as the sun bleached and erased it out.

Chapter Forty-Two

1963 | APRIL

Janet's journey to Holborn had been in relays. The first bus, making an unexpected termination at St Paul's, left her no option but to run for shelter inside the cathedral. Feeling the size of a dormouse, Janet waited for half an hour, praying for the rain to stop. But it wasn't showing any signs of letting up yet. Looking high up into the dome, she thought what a difficult jigsaw it would make.

Along with everybody else escaping the deluge, the Underground was the only resort. But trains and space on them were hard to come. Eventually, arriving at Holborn station, she poked her head out from the awning and contemplated the frantic dash to Wiseman's office a few blocks down on the right.

'Hang on to me, lovey… It's like Noah and his Ark out there. Come on, quick march.' And before Janet knew it, protected by a huge black umbrella, she was being propelled across the road by a crisply wimpled nun, and deposited in the doorway of a large bookshop. As the good sister stepped over the threshold, she gave Janet a no-doubts smile and disappeared inside.

Anyone attempting to leave the shop took one look at the sky and stayed put, scrunching themselves up against her, and as far away from the rain as possible. Janet peered over shoulders and tried to get an eyeful of the monumental building opposite. All day she had fretted about the best way to reach Eileen without being noticed by anyone from Wiseman's. Whatever was going to happen next was going to be terrible. She knew that. Sentences of how to put it, ask it of Eileen, rattled her nerve ends. Rattled her so much that an involuntary noise shuddered from her mouth, and the man next to her gave a cocked ear. As if she had spoken to him.

'Erm, it's half past four,' he said, looking at his wristwatch.

Pointless now. Eileen would have left for home ages ago. Janet, having come this far, knew she would have to commit to something. Chance something. At least cross the road, to find, or wait for, Brian. But she was wedged in.

She had no approachable thoughts, just dots of things that wouldn't join up to anything. Ideas, questions, blanking out before becoming fully formed. Katherine's horrible tidings had made mincemeat of everything.

Janet's brain muddled through pictures of her brothers and sisters, shoving Brian in amongst them. Nothing fitted. Nan and Granddad. Did they know? Had they always known? Mum and Dad. Dad, pretending to be ever so perfect and king of the castle, doing all sorts of grubby things with Eileen, years before. Eileen, her friend and protector... gone down the Swannee along with everybody else. Janet's important safe little gods collapsing like ninepins and leaving her without a life to call her own.

The beat and thrum of the rain dribbled to a full stop, and

the grey streets were lit up by the sparkle of the sun. A communal sigh of relief spread through the doorway, people rearranged their belongings, filtered out, and went on their way.

A tiny dawning, of shackles unlocking, released her towards some embryonic revenge. No matter what happened from this moment on, whether she found Brian, or the truth, there would be no going back. They could search for her all their lives, and so effing what? Without absorbing much of the world around her, Janet stepped on to the pavement, and made three vexed steps to the kerbside. She braced herself for the more than likely humiliations to come, and very alone.

Ben. He would know how to deal with this. The one important person left in her orbit. To Ben's nest she would fly.

The Easter March to look forward to. A student, finally, by proxy.

Fred, turning right from Kingsway, had taken the corner a bit too sharp and fast, and the tyres misbehaved in the wet conditions. Brian spotted Janet, a hundred yards away, standing at the edge of the kerb.

And then she was gone.

Blinded by the sun, Janet's other senses were battered by the stench of burning rubber and the hysterical blast of a motor horn. A painful jolt in the back had pitched and tumbled her, on elbows and knees, into a filthy puddle in the middle of the road. Brian grabbed the wheel, squashing Fred against the side window, and veered the van on to the other side of the road.

Eileen would have seen it speeding towards her, but her view was partially obscured by the back end of a chubby green petrol lorry, and her eyes were fixed on Janet sprawled on the ground.

Further down the road, on the pavement outside his shop, Tony the newsagent was yelling, jumping up and down on the spot, and waving his arms. No one could hear him.

The boom of the first explosion rattled through the innards of everyone in the vicinity. Seconds later, two more blasts, in quick succession.

A heart-beat, and then the gut-wrenching ululations of agony coming from high up.

'My baby... no no no... my baby... my baby... Brian...'

Eileen stretching so far, and almost falling out of the window to reach him, her face contorted with desolation.

The unnatural fireball burning in the hobs of hell beneath was overclouded by thick black smoke that billowed high and wide into the sky. A congregational minute's silence fell over the length and breadth of the street. Hands that had clamped themselves to faces in horror were now giving protection from the putrid fumes.

'I see it... I tell you... I see it. It was her... all her fault.' Tony broke the hush, running towards Janet and the chaos, pointing, 'Her!... her!'

He aimed his fist at the retreating back of a small, ginger-haired woman. She passed the carnage on her left without a glance, swung her furled umbrella, and disappeared into the crowd at the crossroads.

Brian's last blink of life was the advertisement on the side of the petrol tanker.

Chapter Forty-Three

1983 | LONDON

The sun had barely lit the Sunday morning. Also debating what to do next were the low clouds, draping the ceiling of London.

Janet walked a few paces up and down the pavement, looking around, glancing at her watch a few times, scrutinizing the audience of flowers; anything to bring some kind of attention and get served, wishing the stall owner to appear from somewhere soon. It was her third visit in nine months, three touristy weekends away in London, and everything on the list was still unticked off, apart from this place. Only the dead to be spoken to.

She decided to serve herself. Janet dismissed the flowers and their showtime gaudy colours, instead plucked branches of greenery, fronds, grasses and twigs from the back of each of the buckets. Without these props, the flowers flopped and thinly spread themselves, a picture of depressing non-life.

Her dark-green zip-up jump-suit had pockets everywhere: one breast pocket for her passport; one for lipstick and keys; and the two button-down pockets at the sides of her thighs for different languages of money. She double-checked it was English and left the five-pound note under the middle bucket on the second shelf. Too much and yet not enough, she thought.

Among all the other graves, 10-z stood out. Spotlessly gleaming, with, as usual, fresh white lilies in the globe urn. Janet imagined him down there: not a flat-out bony cadaver, but sitting up in the van, laughing and twinkling, his violet eyes full of mischief and life.

'I collided with the world when I collided with you, and for that I am forever grateful. Thank you.'

Her lips barely moving, she decorated leaves in a circle around the outside of the grave, a ritual of crowning him. She got up and drifted through the empty cemetery, wondering how best to fill the afternoon. Aldgate, Holborn, Vauxhall, had all been walked and trawled through. Nothing. And nobody.

The beautiful building of Wiseman's, Luderman's and the bank had metamorphosed into Queen's Arcade, an emporium of high-street fashion on all floors.

Janet had bought the green jump-suit there yesterday, spending time going up and down in the lift and walking through its marble halls, the only bits left alone.

Aldgate seemed very foreign every trip back. Shitty half-demolished warehouses had somehow been scrubbed back into existence as shops, apartments, estate agents. Her flats had gone completely, the people and their memories with them, a mean piece of green in their place, where dossers lay on old newspapers, drinking from cans. Vauxhall had always been the unknown place, and it remained that way.

Coming through the gates, back on to the deserted streets,

Janet didn't know which way to turn. This cemetery was in a slightly awkward part of town, too awkward for her to make up a new jaunt to somewhere. She wasn't dressed for emergency weather, and, at some point this afternoon, that was beginning to feel a highly likely event.

She watched a curly, stumpy black dog on a lead, from one of the terraced houses opposite, drag a young man down the garden path. Following behind and locking up, was a girl of about eighteen, her big red-coated lips giggling and full of fun. There wasn't that much traffic, but a bus suddenly pulling out had to be dodged, and then a fast car coming in the opposite direction. Janet turned away, put her hands over her eyes, her ribs banging. Honking, barking, and squealing broke the Sunday silence.

All three got to the other side of the road in a great rush, the dog yapping itself silly.

'Mind yourself.' She looked back round, and quickly moved out of the way of the spindly tree, where the dog, on one trembly leg, was splashing his pee.

Boy and girl were dressed almost exactly the same, everything as black as their dog: tight jeans, T-shirt, and heavy-shouldered masculine jackets. At top and toe, they went their slightly different ways: spiky-heeled ankle-boots and fluffed-up black hair for her, polished Dr Martens boots for him. He didn't have any hair.

It crossed Janet's mind that the shaved head might be a camouflage, erasing unmentionable ginger hair.

The dog appeared to know exactly where it was going, and heaved on its leash down the side street, by the cemetery. Janet followed to the corner, and saw all three come to a skidding stop at the door of a pub. She imagined them wearing matching outfits forever, moving gently into middle age from black sharpness into colourful saggy tracksuits. A muffled drum of thunder cracked open the clouds and rain started to fall in slow, fat plops. Sheet lightning flickered, some distance away, towards the centre of the city. Janet made a dash for it, shoulders up, pressing her hands tight to both thigh pockets as she sprinted, to keep all the contents under control.

There was nowhere for her to sit down. The one long room was filled with the smell of roasting meat, cabbage and fat, making Janet feel hungry and nauseous at the same time. Beyond the bar, up in the right-hand corner, was a dining area of half a dozen cramped tables, in a small quadrangle. Married-looking couples silently eating, or selecting what to eat, monopolized every space. The black-dressed pair studied the cardboard menu, the little dog mooching round and round under the table.

Janet didn't rattle with aloneness, nor couple-dom, somehow she managed an entry visa into both worlds. A pang of Mum, Katherine and the littlies shot across her bows, and whether they had grown into this release?

Outside, the rain pelted against the crinkly-glassed windows, crackling white light followed seconds later by thunder booms. The barmaid let out a short grating scream which made everyone jump, and patted her heart for quietening and comfort. Then the curly dog barked yappy warnings to all, getting entangled in its leash.

'Oh my life. You're more hysterical than this bloody weather. That noise went right through me.' The bulky hairy waiter, in chef's hat, had pushed himself and two steaming plates of roast dinner through the stable doors behind the bar. He gave an impatient nod towards the bar flap, but the wrinkled blonde barmaid was girlishly simpering with three old geezers leaning on the counter, and didn't notice the command. Janet lifted the flap for him. He marched over to a table and, in an anyhow manner, slapped the food down and almost threw the cutlery at his customers.

'What can I get you, lovey?' The barmaid was still winking and playing with her trio of aged admirers, while tapping her long pink fingernails in front of Janet.

'Mm. Gin and tonic, I think. Thanks.'

'Ice? Lemon?'

Janet felt uncomfortable speaking, and just gave a nod, pushing her fingers through her short bob and rearranging the high straight fringe in the optic-covered mirror opposite. She wanted to ask if there was any bar food going, but her English wasn't naturally dancing around her mind yet.

'Can you allow me to treat you to that, miss?' The old duffer next to her opened an expensive-looking leather wallet. His two chums gave her a wink.

'No. No, you mustn't do that. But thank you.' And she slapped down a note from her pocket. The wrong pocket.

'What's this supposed to be?' The ancient blonde bombshell sneered at the ten-guilder note and gave the perched companions a triumphant 'tut', as if Janet had manufactured it in some den of iniquity.

She resented the blush that crept over her, and snapped into her other self. Taking time to rummage in the other pocket, she said in a small tight accent, 'Mijn fout. I have it,' and handed over a fiver.

Now it was the quartet's turn to shift uncomfortably. She had a flash from years ago, how her mother would nervously negotiate around those from another class, apologizing for her shabby existence. Janet had sloughed off that inheritance twenty years ago.

Outside, the rain was teeming down, and there was nothing else for it but to stay put. Taking her drink and change, without looking up, or bothering much with niceties, she moved away, further down the bar, closer to the tables, nearly colliding with the waiter rushing from the kitchen with two more plates.

The first sip of gin hit the spot where food should have been sitting, and a metallic tang clung to the inside of her mouth. She hadn't eaten anything since last night. Janet scanned the room, hoping for some signs of movement.

The man in the furthest corner wedged himself out and made for the bar, but his companion stayed where she was. 'Two more half Mackeson's, Dolly, when you're ready, love,' he called through to blondie, and laid a pile of small change on the counter. He turned to Janet and both of them laughed at the mountain of cash. 'Looks like I've been robbing fruit machines, don't it?'

'Maybe… Excuse me… are you the flower-man? Outside the cemetery?'

'I am. Take what you want, and leave the money in the tin by the irises. I'll trust you.'

He'd replied automatically, before recalling that queer floating accent. English… yet slightly askew. He gave her face a quick study and darted back to the table; whispered a brief something to his woman, who turned her head and stood up in one mercurial waft.

The twenty-year truancy from each other plonked everything back to who they once were, the pub walls disappearing into a silent kaleidoscope of that street, that day. Time had done a thorough rinse-through of Eileen, and faded her; light-brown soft hair now a perm of iron-grey waves.

'Where have you been? I've been worried sick about you.' Eileen's half-bossy, half-careless note hadn't changed at all. Janet couldn't speak. She stared into a past that had suddenly taken off its stays and didn't render itself such a drama any more.

'I think you should come and sit down before you fall down,' Eileen said. The flower-seller chivvied them to the table and sat them opposite each other.

'He mentioned that some woman was asking for me a while ago... he being my husband here... Sorry, so rude, this is Eddie.'

'Hello,' Janet said.

'I'll see if the drinks have arrived and get myself another chair. Would you like that topped up?' He pointed to Janet's half-swigged gin.

She shook her head, mumbled a 'Thanks' and he left them to it.

Numbed into a 'Where do we start?' the pair of them just sat there, waiting, looking as miserable as sin. Janet constantly rubbed at the gap between her thumb and forefinger until the itching eczema showed signs of weeping. Eileen soaked up the ripe loveliness of the girl across from her, and tried to recapture a portrait of the dead.

Eddie broke into this with his chair and drinks. 'Can you

remember what he looked like? Really looked like? Could you conjure him up, sitting here now, with us?' Eileen's thought swam out of her mouth.

Eddie could see that Janet wasn't sure which way to answer this for the best. 'Come on, Eileen, one at a time. She's not answered your first question yet. Like, where have you been?' He made it sound as if they had all met up again at a wedding party or school reunion, and were doing polite catch-up.

'Your dad came to see me when you didn't go back that night. I know you've never been home…' Eileen waited, but got nothing. 'He kept coming round, every Sunday in that first year. You broke their hearts, as sure as he broke mine. Anyway, once your family knew for sure that we weren't hiding you, he stopped; would write from time to time… just to see if I had heard anything. When I moved, what, twelve months ago? I didn't forward any address, to anybody in fact.'

Janet thought of Katherine, the littlies, her mum and dad. Imagining them exactly the same. Now, meeting Eileen, the gone years were underlined with a vengeance, the mental arithmetic too easy. Everyone grown up… or dead.

She spread her hand and looked at the eczema. It had stopped itching. 'I ran away to Holland with a boy. The first three years I was too scared to come back. After that, I was too different to come back.'

'We're all different eventually,' Eileen said. She leant across and lifted Janet's hand; examined the soreness and gave it a couple of little pats. 'Do you have any kids?'

Janet shook her head and swallowed the last of her gin.

'When Eddie told me a woman was asking for me, my first thought was that Ginger Nuts. Remember her? I wonder where she is now? Little Miss Muffet, still probably sitting on her poncy tuffet somewhere, causing trouble.'

'I dream about those times every now and again, you and Brian. Almost as much these days as I did in the beginning.' Janet looked to Eddie while she said this.

'Well, I reckon you must think of him every time you look in the mirror. You're the little twin of him. Different colour in the eyes, of course. His peepers must have been some sort of throwback, a lucky draw, from history.'

And that was what let the air in. This had never really been about a kids' romance, or the lazy untruths. The handcuffs for all three of them had been about a disastrous togetherness: the deeds to Brian rented out for morality's sake, and Eileen's most precious thing stolen forever.

The pub was beginning to empty, glasses and plates collected, the clink and smack of business coming to a stop. Eddie told them to stay where they were, he would get back to the cemetery and hopefully see them around four.

'Happy anniversary,' he said as he clinked an empty beer glass with Eileen. 'The first of many, we hope.'

'It's alright, we can stay as long as we like. Me and Eddie live in the house next door. They'll just lock us in. Fancy another?'

'Do I really look like him?'